UNDENIABLE

"So this is where you've been hiding," a deep male voice said. Startled, she looked up to see a man standing in the doorway. He walked toward her and into the light where she could see his face clearly. His hair flowed about his shoulders. He was by far the most handsome man she'd ever laid eyes on, she thought, as his deep-set black eyes assessed her. His pictures hadn't done him justice. She wanted to touch him to see if he was real.

"Zander?"

"Mara?" He stopped and she had to tilt her head back to meet his gaze. His eyes intensified as they held hers.

"It's nice to finally put a face with the name."

"Same here," he said in a rich baritone that sent shivers down her spine. She drew a deep breath as he took her hand—his was large and warm. Mara had never been instantly attracted to a man before. She wondered what he would look like without the shirt. What was she thinking? She had taken one look at him and wanted him on the spot—and on top of that, he was her best friend's brother. This was not good.

UNDENIABLE

Ingrid Monique

Dafina
Books

Kensington Publishing Corp.
http://www.kensingtonbooks.com

DAFINA BOOKS are published by

Kensington Publishing Corp.
850 Third Avenue
New York, NY 10022

All Kensington titles, imprints and distributed lines are available at special quantity discounts for bulk purchases for sales promotion, premiums, fund-raising, educational or institutional use.

Special book excerpts or customized printings can also be created to fit specific needs. For details, write or phone the office of the Kensington Special Sales Manager: Kensington Publishing Corp., 850 Third Avenue, New York, NY 10022. Attn. Special Sales Department. Phone: 1-800-221-2647.

Dafina and the Dafina logo Reg. U.S. Pat. & TM Off.

First Printing: March 2005
10 9 8 7 6 5 4 3 2 1

Printed in the United States of America

Chapter 1

Mara Evans zipped her small suitcase shut and turned to her mother. Janice Evans was a short, chocolate-colored woman in her late fifties, with large brown eyes and a gentle smile. She had been born on the island of St. Thomas in the Caribbean.

"You sure you want me to go?" Mara asked, worried.

"Me fine. Yu' jus' to go an' enjoy yu'self." Janice told her. Janice had lived in the States for the past twenty years and had never lost her accent.

Mara was apprehensive about leaving her mother alone for two months. The longest they had ever been apart was a few days. Mara was very protective of her mother, because it had been just the two of them for the past nineteen years. Her father walked out on them when she was only six. They depended on each other for everything. What would her mother do without her? Mara knew she was having separation issues, but she couldn't help it. As much as she needed this vacation, she didn't want to leave her mother.

Mara looked at her mother, suddenly unsure. "I think I should stay," Mara insisted.

"No, yu' not! Yu goin' to New Jersey an' yu' goin' to have a good time."

"But Mama . . ."

"Don't start again," Janice said, rolling her eyes.

"Won't you miss me?" Mara pouted, and her mother smiled, then put on her serious face.

"What I jus' say?"

"OK." Mara gave up and hugged her mother.

"Yu' need to have some fun for a change." Janice kissed her cheek and hugged her.

Mara would be in New Jersey for the next two months, vacationing at her best friend Shari Tuskcan's home. Her vacation would be topped off with her being Shari's maid of honor her last week there. Mara was looking forward to Shari's wedding, but she had no idea what she would do for two months. Two months of doing nothing would probably drive her crazy. Relax and enjoy, she reminded herself. This would be her first real vacation. Mara had never taken a vacation; it just wasn't something she did. Any free time she had, she worked to help her mother out. Mara had been working since she was sixteen.

Mara pulled back and looked at her mother, who had moved to the United States when she was nineteen. Janice had worked as a live-in maid to a distant cousin for years until she met her future husband. Hard work and stress had turned her mother's hair prematurely white. Mara touched her mother's soft hair; she had been trying to get her mother to dye it for years. Of course, she refused, claiming she preferred it the way it was.

Mara was the very image of her mother, with her small, round nose, full, almost-round lips, and big, dark-brown eyes. They both stood at five-two and wore the same size, eight. The only thing Mara hadn't inherited from her mother was her curly West Indian hair. Mara's hair was thick and unruly; she wore it cut in a short bob.

For the past twenty years Janice had worked as a custodian for Howard University. At first, Mara had hated the fact that her mother worked so hard, but that job had enabled her to earn a college degree through tuition remission and scholarships. A part of her couldn't wait to start her career as a programmer and take care of her mother. She wanted her mother to retire—landing a good job would ensure that. With her degree and the market today, she knew she would do well.

Mara scanned the living room of the two-bedroom apartment she and her mother had lived in for the past nine years in the three-story walk-up on Irving Street. Their apartment was warm and cozy and very lived-in. They could use some new furniture, but that would come in time.

The doorbell rang, pulling Mara out of her musing; she answered it, expecting Shari. But it was Henry Johnson, a member of their church and a very good friend of her mother's. He lived in a historic house right across the street.

Henry was in his late fifties, a handsome man with caramel skin and light-green eyes. He was a looker, and just about every woman, young and old, noticed him. He had lost his wife five years ago to cancer. Somehow he gravitated toward Janice. Mara figured it was her mother's cooking that brought him over most of the time.

Henry flashed a charming smile. "I hear some-one's off to New Jersey."

"Mom told you that quick?"

Mara gazed at her mother as Henry entered the apartment, closing the door behind him.

"Hush," Janice said playfully.

"I see you're all set," Henry said, looking at her suitcase and backpack.

"Yeah."

"You deserve it. You've worked hard all these years. Enjoy it."

"Yu' tell her," Janice chimed in. Before Mara could respond, the doorbell rang. Mara rushed to the door—this time it was Shari.

Shari was a stunning African/Native American woman, tall and thin with bronze skin and light-brown eyes. Her long hair fell in waves down her back. Mara recalled seeing Shari for the first time in freshman English class and thinking she had to be a model. Shari had an impeccable sense of style, a bit classic with a trendy twist. Today she was dressed in a long, powder-blue linen dress and a matching cardigan thrown over her shoulders.

While she and Shari were complete opposites, from their lifestyles to their backgrounds, they had somehow formed a lasting, close friendship.

"Ready?" Shari stepped into the apartment.

"Oh, yeah." Mara was unable to hide her excitement.

Shari hugged Janice and shook Henry's hand.

"Thanks for takin' her," Janice said. Mara rolled her eyes.

"Mama!"

"An' please make sure she enjoy' herself."

"Mama," Mara moaned, embarrassed.

"Trust me, she will," Shari said.

Henry moved to pick up her case. "I got it, Henry," she insisted.

"No, please let me." Henry took her case outside.

"I'll be downstairs," Shari said, picking up her backpack.

Mara turned to her mother, who opened her arms with a smile as Mara rushed to her. She took a mental note of her mother's fresh scent of Irish Spring soap and floral body splash.

"I want you to enjoy yu'self, yu' hear me? An' don't worry 'bout me. I'll be fine."

"Sure?"

"Yes." Janice kissed her cheek. "Now come. Shari' waiting."

A private car waited out front to take them to the airport.

"Don't you worry, I'll take care of Janice for you," Henry said as he gave Mara a hug. Mara thanked him, then hugged and kissed her mother one last time before she got into the car.

As they drove off, she looked back to see her mother and Henry—he had his arm around her mother's waist as they waved good-bye. She waved back, sighed, and settled back against the seat. She would not cry. She would enjoy her vacation.

"Glad to see you smiling. I was afraid you'd start crying on me. Or even worse, change your mind," Shari said.

"Have you ever seen me cry?"

"No, but you came close a couple of times."

"OK, then." Mara tried to maintain a serious expression.

"It's going to be fun. You'll see."

"I'm looking forward to it." And she really was. It felt good to finally let go of her worries for a change.

Chapter 2

The plane ride from National Airport to Newark, New Jersey, took about an hour. A private car picked them up and headed to Spring Lake, where Shari lived. The minute Mara was settled into the back of the car she fell asleep.

"We're home," Shari said and shook her awake sometime later.

Mara blinked the sleep from her eyes. The driver opened the car door, and Shari got out first. Mara covered a yawn and followed. What Mara saw as she stepped from the car took her breath away: a white, three-story mansion with rising pillars. Marble steps led to a stained-glass door. The grounds surrounding the house were blooming with flower paths. She could see other lavish homes in the distance.

"Welcome to my home." Shari smiled.

"This is not your house!" Mara said in disbelief.

"Yes, it is," Shari said. "Now stop gawking and come along." Shari took her by the arm and pulled her up the stairs to the front door. Mara knew Shari's family had money and expected her to live in a nice house, but this was unbelievable. Then again, Shari was the only student she knew in D.C. who drove the latest BMW and lived in a condo on Connecticut Avenue, in one of the most expensive neighborhoods.

Mara stopped midway up the stairs, suddenly overwhelmed. Shari turned and frowned at her.

"What now?"

"You should have warned me."

"About what?"

"All this."

"Would you stop—and come along?" Shari pulled at her. Mara went along, wondering what the interior looked like. Gorgeous, no doubt.

A short, brown-skinned African-American woman opened the front door as they approached. She was in her early fifties with salt-and-pepper hair. She had a sweet, kind face with expressive, welcoming black eyes. Mara knew it was Helen.

"Helen!" Shari cried, and flew into the woman's open arms.

Helen had been with the family since Shari was born. She was designated guardian to Shari and her brother Zander after their parents died. She had talked to Helen on the phone over the years and found her to be warm and sincere.

Helen smiled at her. "Mara?" she asked. Mara nodded. Helen pulled her into her arms and hugged her warmly. Helen smelled of baked goods and fragrant flowers.

"It's so good to finally meet you," Helen said.

"Same here, and thanks for having me," Mara said.

"It's our pleasure—come inside." Helen ushered them in. Mara followed her into the foyer. There was a modern oak table accented by a large vase of fresh tulips. The scent of the flowers filled the room, and Mara took in a deep breath. A curved oak staircase led upstairs. Mara couldn't help feeling as if she had just stepped into the pages of *Décor* magazine.

"So, how was the flight?" Helen asked, as she led them into the lavish living room, decorated in cream and peach. A huge fireplace stood at the head of the room, exquisite paintings hung on the walls. Very modern with a touch of classic.

"It was OK," Shari answered, as Mara continued to admire the room. She noticed a portrait of Shari's parents over the fireplace and decided to take a closer look. Except for the hair, Shari looked just like her mother.

"You look just like your mother," Mara commented.

"Is Zander here?" Shari asked Helen.

"Yes, he's home. He said he'd be home for dinner."

"Good, I'm glad he's here."

"Why don't you two go freshen up. Dinner will be ready in fifteen minutes," Helen told them.

"Thanks, Helen."

"Thank you," Mara said as Helen left the room.

Mara knew that Shari and her brother didn't have the best relationship. In the four years that Shari had been in D.C., Zander never visited his sister. He wasn't even at Shari's graduation. Shari never talked much about him except to paint him as a cold-hearted businessman. She had always wondered what had put that distance between them.

Mara picked up a picture of Shari and Zander off the mantel. Shari was smiling and Zander had a stern look on his chiseled, handsome bronze face.

His eyes were lifeless and unhappy in a way that made her wonder what he was thinking at the time.

"What's with you and your brother, anyway?" She replaced the picture and turned to Shari.

"He's all about money. Nothing else—or no one—matters to him."

"Come on, he can't be that bad."

"Wait till you meet him. Come on, let's go get ready for dinner."

Mara was very impressed by her room. It was large and very cozy, decorated in lavender and cream with a king-size sledge bed. A painting depicting a landscape hung above the fireplace. Fresh flowers were by the bed, filling the room with a wonderful aroma. French windows lured her out onto the balcony that overlooked the gardens and a swimming pool. The view beyond was even more spectacular, with a lush landscape that disappeared into the surrounding woods. The cool summer breeze caressed her face. She was definitely not in D.C. anymore.

"Now, this is a bathroom," Mara said aloud as she entered the bathroom. There was a large, claw-footed tub in the middle of the room—off to the side was a glass shower. She freshened up and changed into a T-shirt and mid-calf skirt. She was about to leave her room but decided to call her mother.

"Hello," her mother answered.

"Hi, Mama," she sang into the phone.

"Yu' reach OK?"

"Yes, you should see this place—it's like a palace."

"Yu' jus' enjoy yu'self," Janice reminded her.

"I intend to. Miss me yet?" Mara teased.

"Of course me miss me baby." It made Mara smile.

"I miss you, too."

"Well, don't miss me too much an' enjoy yu'self."

"OK, Mama."

"Luv' yu'."

"Love you, too. I'll call you in a few days."

"Make it next week—Henry takin' me an' Joyce to Baltimore Harbor."

"Have fun."

"Yu' too, baby, talk to yu' soon, an' tell Shari I said hello."

"I will."

She said good-bye and hung up the phone. Mara was glad that her mother wasn't missing her. It would make being here so long a bit easier. She left her room to see Shari coming out of hers, which was across the hall.

"So do you like your room?" Shari asked as they headed downstairs.

"Are you kidding? I've never been in a room that luxurious before. This whole palace is a dream. I can't wait to see the rest of it."

"It's not a palace," Shari laughed.

"Trust me. This is a palace to me."

"I want you to feel at home—no worrying about anything. Just sit back, relax, and enjoy."

"What else can I do?" This was a fantasy vacation for her, and she intended to enjoy it. "Mama says hello."

"She's not missing you too much, is she?" Shari asked, concerned.

"Nope, Mr. Johnson's taking her and Joyce to Baltimore Harbor."

"Sounds like fun."

In the kitchen Helen had plates of steaming food ready for them. After a dinner of roast chicken with baby potatoes and vegetables, Mara and Shari lounged by the pool with glasses of white wine. *Now this is the life*, Mara mused. She'd never been this relaxed, and it felt good. Real good. She was glad she had decided to come to New Jersey. Definitely.

"I'm going to walk this dinner off." Mara got up, stretching. She felt a bit sluggish.

"Don't get lost," Shari teased, as she headed inside.

"If you hear me screaming, come get me."

Chapter 3

The house had three floors. The top two were all bedrooms; the main floor housed the dining room, living room, and kitchen, with a small dining area to its right. There was also an entertainment room with plush sofas and a giant flat-screen TV mounted on the wall.

There was also a library/home office, which Shari fell in love with. It was furnished in rich, dark oak, giving the room a warm, cozy feel. French windows looked out into the gardens. Massive bookcases lined the walls. There was a fireplace and a small bar. Noticing a large picture book depicting Native American art on the coffee table, Mara sat down and flipped through it.

"So this is where you've been hiding," a deep male voice said. Startled, she looked up to see a man standing in the doorway. He walked toward her and into the light where she could see his face clearly. His hair flowed about his shoulders. He was by far the most handsome man she'd ever laid eyes on. He was tall, well over six feet—about six-six, she guessed. Deep-set black eyes boldly assessed her; his pictures hadn't done him any justice at all. He was absolutely fine. He smiled and Mara suddenly went blank. She stared openly at him. His face was chiseled to perfection, with high cheekbones, sexy, full lips, and a sharp nose. His skin was a flawless bronze. She wanted to touch him to see if he was real.

A part of Mara had expected a hard-looking man dressed in a suit. But there was nothing hard about his warm, smiling eyes. He wore loose slacks and a linen shirt with sandals. The man oozed sexuality.

"Zander?"

"Mara?" He stopped in front of her and she had to tilt her head to meet his gaze. His eyes intensified as they held hers.

"It's nice to finally put a face with the name."

"Same here," he said in a deep baritone that sent shivers down her spine. She took a deep breath as he took her hand—his was large and warm. Her eyes traveled up to his biceps. Nice. Real nice. She wondered what he would look like without the shirt. What was she thinking? He was Shari's brother. Mara had never been instantly attracted to any man before. She had taken one look at him and wanted him on the spot, and on top of all that, he was her best friend's brother. This was not good.

Zander found himself staring at Mara. Her full lips were perfectly round. Her big, brown eyes held him captive. He liked the roundness of her features; they made her adorable. Her face was makeup-free and flawless, adding to her natural beauty. Her short hair was brushed back against her scalp. She looked up at him with curiosity. He noted how short she was—she barely reached his shoulders. He allowed his eyes to slowly assess her curvaceous frame—her well-defined legs and arms, her small breasts and slim waist. She was definitely not the kind of woman he was usually attracted to. He liked his women tall and thin, model-like. Mara smiled and moistened her lips, and he became instantly aroused. He reminded himself that she was Shari's friend. He wondered what she would taste like. He cleared his throat and refocused his thoughts.

"I hope you don't mind my looking around. You have a beautiful home." Mara forced her thoughts away from his overwhelming sexuality. His eyes had just finished assessing her, and she had grown warm under his gaze. She felt her nipples harden and a heat began to rise deep within her.

"Thank you, and no, I don't mind. Make yourself at home." His eyes darkened and she knew his thoughts were similar to hers. It sent shivers down her spine. He could make a woman melt with just one look. A caution light went on in Mara's head—lusting after Shari's brother was not cool.

"Thank you." She wondered what it would be like to kiss those sexy lips. He was probably a good kisser. What was she thinking?

"Good, you two found each other." Shari poked her head in the doorway, and Mara was glad for the distraction. She tried to focus on Shari. "Helen's pie is ready."

"After you." Zander allowed her to move past him. She caught a whiff of his cologne. Not only did he look good, he smelled good.

Mara sat beside Shari at the kitchen island over pie and tea while Zander sat at the other end. Mara tried her best not to stare at him, but it was hard. The man was too fine. She had seen fine men before, but there was something about this man that had captured her interest.

"Have you spoken to Patrick since you've been back?" Zander asked Shari.

"He's in Boston," Shari answered.

Mara knew Zander was about thirty-one or so and he was single. She wondered if he had a woman. Shari had told her he was briefly married once. He had it annulled after he found out his wife was after his money. How much had he loved his ex-wife, and how much had she hurt him? She wondered what kind of effect it had on him.

"Kate's birthday party is Sunday. You two should go," Zander said, looking at Mara. She looked away at Shari. She could feel his eyes on her.

"Aren't you coming?" Shari asked tentatively.

"I have meetings and a late dinner that day." Mara saw disappointment fill Shari's eyes. Shari pushed her plate away.

"So this party—is it going to be any fun?" Mara asked, trying to cheer up Shari.

"Of course," Shari beamed. "I can't wait for you to meet Kate. She's wonderful. She's been helping me plan the wedding."

Zander's cell phone rang, halting the conversation. Zander answered his phone on the second ring.

"Hello, yes, one second," he said. "Excuse me, ladies, I have to take this call. And Shari—" Shari turned to look at him, annoyed. He didn't seem to notice. "Tanya and I are engaged, in case Helen hasn't told you yet," he informed her and calmly left the room, the phone at his ear. Helen returned to the kitchen and started to clear the dishes.

So he had a fiancée? Of course he did. A man like Zander wouldn't be without a woman. She was probably drop-dead gorgeous.

"Why didn't you tell me?" Shari asked Helen, devastated.

"What?" Helen said.

"Zander and Tanya, engaged?"

"It's not my place," Helen responded gently.

"Not your place? Helen, you tell me everything." Shari was obviously upset by the news. "Why did you hide this from me? How long has this been going on?"

"Four months."

"Four months!" Shari exhaled, disgusted.

"OK, who is this Tanya?" Mara asked. Shari and Helen looked at her.

"His worst nightmare. I can't believe he's seeing her. What is he thinking?"

"He's been talking about settling down," Helen said.

"So he's going to settle for her?" Shari exploded. Mara had never seen Shari so upset. Shari was always so calm about everything. "He doesn't love her and she sure as hell doesn't love him."

"I've tried telling him that, but he wouldn't listen to me," Helen sighed. "Maybe he'll listen to you."

"Me? Zander doesn't even talk to me. He shuts me out every chance he gets."

"Then what can we do?" Helen said, defeated.

Shari suddenly turned to Mara. "What do you think?" She looked at Shari, baffled.

"What?" Mara blinked. She didn't know Zander well enough to give an opinion on the matter, and even if she did, it was none of her business.

"Breaking up Zander and Tanya," Shari continued with such ease Mara was stunned for a moment.

"What?" Mara couldn't believe what she was asking.

"Come on, Mara, help us out here," Shari pleaded.

"I don't think so."

"She's not right for him."

"Don't tell *me* that, tell him," Mara suggested.

Helen shook her head and said, "Wish it was that easy."

Mara found Shari staring at her intensely. "I don't know Zander or this Tanya woman and I'm not getting involved with your drama," Mara said.

Shari rolled her eyes in frustration. "I just can't believe this! How can he be so blind? He knows her. He knows better."

"I'm sure he knows what he's doing," Mara commented.

"Let's hope so," Helen said doubtfully.

"I'd rather see him alone for the rest of his life than with her," Shari exclaimed with contempt.

Mara wondered how bad Tanya could be for Shari to dislike her so intensely.

Chapter 4

Zander had heard someone come downstairs. Hoping it was Shari so he could talk to her before he left for his office in the morning, he made his way into the kitchen. He stopped short when he saw her. Mara had her head in the refrigerator. She was bent from the waist, her behind in the air. She wore a short cotton nightgown that had little yellow faded flowers. He couldn't help but assess her assets, especially from the rear. She had a nice, round behind. She shifted and one of her nightgown straps fell down her shoulder and he got a nice view of one of her small breasts. Way too small for his taste, but they would fit nicely in the palm of his hand.

A jolt of raw desire raced through his body, shocking him. He blinked and focused. She wasn't his type—why the sudden attraction? He recalled thinking she was cute when he first saw her in the library, but this sudden attraction took him by surprise. He couldn't really be attracted to her, but the heat in his lower body told him differently. She wasn't high-maintenance, nor was she tall or blond: she was not his type.

She reached into the refrigerator, pushing something aside, and her nightgown went up even more, affording him a glimpse of her red panties. He wanted to move up behind her and touch her. Stop! He had to get a grip.

"Looking for something in particular?" He quickly pulled his eyes from her rear.

She jumped, almost dropping the cup in her hand. He hadn't meant to frighten her. Then again, he didn't want her to find him staring at her the way he just was.

"Oh God, you almost scared me to death." She put a hand against her chest and straightened up. He hadn't meant to frighten her. He watched her closely as she closed the refrigerator door and adjusted the strap of her nightgown, cutting off his view of her breasts. She hadn't even realized that she was exposed. She moved toward him, her smile taking his breath away. She was even shorter barefoot, he realized, as he looked down at her. Her short hair was ruffled and he had the strongest urge to smooth it down. "I didn't think anyone would be up," she said, putting her mug on the counter. Her big, brown eyes held him captive. She tilted her head, looking into his eyes. He felt like she was seeing right into his soul. It wasn't something that any woman had made him feel before.

"I had to look over some documents for tomorrow," he volunteered.

"It *is* tomorrow," she said, her gaze taking him all in. He liked the way she looked at him. Open, no fear.

"That it is." He couldn't stop the smile that touched his lips. She shifted, and her small breasts bounced under her nightgown. Her nipples had lost their hardness and it disappointed him, to his surprise. He didn't even like small-breasted women. She was too small. Get a grip! She was his sister's best friend.

"I thought I'd get some warm milk."

"Couldn't sleep?"

"Something like that." She appeared a bit embarrassed.

"You can move to another room if you want."

"The room's fine. I just can't seem to fall asleep." She shrugged and bit into her lower lip.

He wanted to kiss her. He wanted to taste those full, dark, round lips of hers. He knew she'd taste good. But she was his sister's best friend. She was off limits.

"Have a drink with me?" he offered, knowing that a strong drink would put her to sleep faster than the milk.

"What are we having?" She smiled, and for a moment he went blank.

He focused. "Cognac."

"Never had one, but I'll try it."

"You don't drink much, do you?"

"No."

"Good, then the cognac will help you sleep."

"Sounds good to me." Her big eyes sparkled with interest. She could be a problem—a good problem, he thought, looking at her lips.

"Have a seat," he told her as they entered the library. He felt the heat of her body as she moved past him. He poured them both a drink and turned to her. He froze in his tracks. What he saw took his breath away.

She was sitting on the sofa, her legs tucked under her. Her nightgown had shifted, offering him a nice view of her strong thighs. He wondered if she knew just how inviting she looked sitting there. She held a hand out for the drink and he handed her the glass. She took it and gazed into the dark liquid. She sniffed it before taking a sip. He watched as the cognac hit her and she cringed. She was adorable.

"Small sips," he told her, hiding a smile.

"This is strong, but good," she said, licking her lips. Zander sat across from her, studying her closely. Her natural, easy beauty was intoxicating. Nothing was false about her, not even the play of emotions as she sipped the cognac. He took a long sip of his drink.

"So if it's not the room, what's keeping you a-wake?"

She swallowed and licked her lips. "I'm used to hearing snoring in the next room. It puts me to sleep," she admitted.

"Snoring puts you to sleep?"

"My mother's, actually."

He was definitely intrigued by her openness. "You're close to your mother?"

"Yeah."

"Sounds like you miss her."

"I do," she admitted honestly. "We've never really been apart. Ever since my father walked out on us." She suddenly stopped speaking, staring into her glass, obviously recalling some painful memories. Then, just as suddenly, she looked at him, her eyes showing no evidence of pain. He wondered how much her father's leaving had hurt her. Shari had told him that Mara was from a single-parent home. She took a longer sip of the cognac and coughed. Zander chuckled and she looked at him with narrowed eyes.

"So you find me funny?" She eyed him over the glass. From the glassy look in her eyes, he knew she was getting buzzed.

"No, I find you delightful," he told her.

Mara felt herself blush at Zander's compliment. The cognac had her feeling relaxed; she was enjoying Zander's company, to her surprise. The fact that he was so fine was a plus. Of course, he was too fine and too rich for her blood. But who was to say she couldn't enjoy his company?

"In such a short time?"

His dark eyes held hers, warming her even more than the cognac already had.

"I can see why my sister likes you."

"Really?"

"Do you question everything?"

"Just about."

He laughed, and his rich, deep laughter filled the room. Mara liked the way his laughter sounded.

"So can I ask you a question?" she asked.

"Go ahead."

"Why didn't you ever come to D.C. to visit Shari?"

His face suddenly went blank. "I'm a busy man," he responded dryly.

"Too busy for the important things in life?" she asked and watched his expression darken even more. "She wanted you at her graduation. She was really disappointed when you didn't show."

He shifted and cleared his throat. "Shari knew I couldn't make it. I was in Atlanta on business."

Mara studied his cold, defensive body language before responding. "She told me you were all about business."

"Did she, now?"

"Well, aren't you?" she pressed.

"She understands." His eyes hardened.

"No, she doesn't. She wanted you there and you weren't and she was hurt by it."

"She never said anything to me."

"Why should she, when all you do is push her away. Not exactly brotherly of you." Mara had tried to hold her tongue, but just couldn't.

"Why does all this concern you?" he growled. He was impossible, and starting to resemble the picture that Shari had painted of him.

Mara got up, "Thanks for the drink. Good night." She put down her glass and abruptly left the room. Mara climbed the stairs, annoyed mostly at the fact that she found Zander attractive despite his cold, noncaring manner toward his sister. He really was something.

She had just left his library, and left him stunned. Zander was suddenly annoyed and turned on at the same time. How the hell was that possible? He poured himself another drink. Who the hell was she to question his relationship with his sister? Everything was fine between him and Shari. So why was he suddenly feeling guilty? He knew she'd be trouble, with her big, brown eyes and full, round lips. She wasn't even his type of woman. So why the hell was he so turned on by her? He abandoned his drink and headed up to bed.

Only he couldn't seem to sleep, he kept seeing Mara's questioning eyes and those damn lips of hers.

Chapter 5

Mara couldn't remember the last time she had slept so late. She recalled her conversation with Zander and came up with the conclusion that he was a hard-hearted man who saw things only his way. Which made her wonder if he even had a heart. Men like Zander were dangerous for any woman. He was far too fine and far too heartless. Deciding not to give him a second thought, Mara got up, took a shower, dressed, and headed downstairs. She found Helen and Shari by the pool. She was thankful when she saw fruit, muffins, and coffee on the table. She was starving.

"Morning," she greeted them as she took a seat and reached for a blueberry muffin.

"Slept OK?" Helen asked.

"Yes, I did." Mara poured some coffee.

"Good, because we need to go shopping for Kate's party," Shari informed her.

Mara paused. "I don't have any money to go shopping."

Shari rolled her eyes. "Like I said, and don't make me repeat myself, you do not have to worry about anything while you are here."

"But . . ."

"No buts and no objections. You are going to be here for a while. All I want you to do is relax and enjoy yourself for a change."

"Just don't spend too much on me," she insisted softly.

"Would you stop?" Shari rolled her eyes again.

"OK." Mara humbled herself.

Shari had always been generous to her, helping her pay for her books in college when she was short. Mara wasn't a hundred percent comfortable with Shari spending money on her, but she also didn't want to make a fuss. Shari had always been too generous, and as far as she was concerned, had given her enough already.

Shari took her downtown to Spring Lake, where they shopped at the most exquisite boutiques. Mara admired the turn-of-the-century architecture and the warm, family-oriented atmosphere of the town. This was definitely a great place to raise a family. Of course, Shari ended up buying her more clothes than she needed. Mara did her best not to object, knowing Shari would get upset. And with the number of places and parties that Shari had mentioned, she knew she'd need the clothes.

After shopping they had dinner at an Italian restaurant named Jo's. Shari had pasta and grilled salmon and she had the grilled chicken on a bed of angel hair pasta. A group of businessmen at a table across from them reminded Mara of her conversation with Zander earlier that morning.

"I had a little talk with your brother last night."

"Really? About what?"

"I think I upset him, actually." She recalled the look on his face as she walked out of his library.

"You did?"

"I asked him why he wasn't at your graduation."

"And what did he say?" Shari's interest was piqued.

"That he was out of town on business and that you understood."

Shari shook her head. "That's always his excuse. I wonder if he's even going to be at my wedding."

"You don't think he'll be there?" Mara looked at her friend, concerned.

"You never know with him. Like I said, his business comes before everything." Shari frowned.

"Come on, he can't be that bad." Mara sipped her iced tea.

"You want to know why I ended up in D.C.?"

Mara put down her glass and looked at her, waiting for the answer. She had always known Shari wasn't into college. She barely passed her electives, only excelling in her art classes. Shari wasn't exactly interested in college, although she'd earned a degree in Art History.

"I was running away."

"From what?"

"My marriage to Patrick."

Mara almost choked. "You're kidding right?" The people at the next table looked interested in their conversation.

"No. I was running away from my marriage," Shari told her, dead serious.

Mara stared at her, shocked. "Why?"

"Our families have been business associates for years. So when Patrick took an interest in me, Zander insisted that we get married. I grew up having such a crush on Patrick, and I wasn't about to refuse him. I was in heaven until I found out that Patrick's interest in me was more about bringing our families' businesses together than it was about love. That's when I left for Howard."

"I can't believe your marriage is about business." Mara stared at Shari in total disbelief, unable to wrap her mind around what she was hearing.

"Initially, it was."

"And now?"

"I'm marrying Patrick because I love him."

"I know that, but what about him?"

"Back then I wasn't sure if he felt the same way about me, which led to my decision to go to Howard. I wanted to know if he was enough in love with me to wait four years, and he did." Shari grinned. "You know, I left two weeks before the wedding."

"Oh, Zander must have loved that." Mara chuckled sarcastically, picturing Zander losing his cool.

"He didn't speak to me for a year. Even when I was home on breaks, he was always off on some business trip." Sadness filled Shari's eyes.

"That's why you think he won't be at your wedding?"

"Let me put it this way. I want him there, but I don't expect him to show up."

"That's not good." Mara felt bad for her friend. "Have you ever told him why you left?"

"Never had the chance to. He's never available."

"No wonder he got all upset when I started in on him about missing your graduation."

"Now you understand," Shari said sadly, wiping the corners of her mouth with her napkin.

"I guess, but what if you weren't in love with Patrick and didn't want to marry him?"

"Zander would force me to marry Patrick anyway."

"Force you to?" Mara was shocked and appalled. "Shari, no one should be forced into anything, much less marriage."

"I guess it's a good thing that I love Patrick."

"Are you telling me that you would marry him regardless?"

"Yes."

Mara stared at her, stunned. "I guess it's a good thing you do love him."

"I do." Shari eyes sparkled.

Mara sighed, looking at Shari. A part of her couldn't help but worry about her. Mara took comfort in the fact that Shari was in love with Patrick. She had seen them together over the years, and Patrick seemed to love her. She prayed that his love for Shari was real.

Chapter 6

For Shari's future mother-in-law's birthday party, Mara wore a black strapless, mid-calf rayon dress and high-heeled black pumps. She had wrapped and brushed her hair so it fell in smooth layers about her head. She admired her new look in the mirror, pleased with what she saw. She had definitely never looked so sophisticated or beautiful, and she liked it. Excited, she rushed into Shari's room to see if she was ready.

Shari looked her over. "Looking good."

"I feel like Cinderella." Mara looked down at her dress, smoothing her hand over the cool fabric, loving the way it accentuated her figure.

"Cinderella ain't got nothing on you." Shari said.

She did look good and it felt good. She was going to have fun tonight.

Shari wore a long, one-shouldered red dress that fell to her ankles, accentuated by a thigh-high slit. Mara had done her hair in a French twist, with a few ringlets at her temples.

Shari walked over to her jewelry box and opened it, pulling out a ruby necklace and matching drop earrings.

"Wear these." She handed them to Mara, who took the jewelry and stared at the sparkling jewels. "I . . ."

"Don't start, just put them on," Shari said, cutting her off.

Mara took off her only piece of jewelry, a pair of gold stud earrings, and put the new ones on. "These are nice," Mara said.

"They look good on you," Shari said. "We have to go or we'll be fashionably late."

Mara stepped from the Town Car and was stunned by the Rhone mansion. It was turn-of-the-century in design and absolutely magnificent. They had some major money. A large antique fountain with water cascading into the air from a nymph's flute stood before the mansion. Mara felt like she was going to a ball as she watched well-dressed couples make their way into the mansion. Shari took her arm and led her toward the entrance. Suddenly she felt a bit overwhelmed and out of place. She instantly reminded herself that she was here to have fun. She was going to enjoy it all.

A doorman dressed in a tux greeted them on their way inside. Mara barely caught a glimpse of the stunning foyer as Shari hurried her along into a grand ballroom. People were scattered around the room, as waiters moved among them with silver trays of champagne and hors d'oeuvres. They had been in the main room for less than a minute when someone called out to Shari.

Mara watched as a handsome young man with a

caramel complexion and light hazel eyes moved to embrace Shari warmly.

"Welcome, welcome!" he said as he looked over at Mara and took her hand. "And who is this?" He kissed the back of Mara's hand. Up close, his eyes were absolutely stunning. He was cute.

"Franklin, this is Mara. Mara, Franklin, Patrick's younger brother."

He was cute but too young. Mara smiled.

"It's so nice to meet you, Mara."

"Nice to meet you, too, Franklin."

Franklin held out both his arms, and they took them.

"Come, Mother will be so happy to see you." He led them into the ballroom, and Mara found herself being introduced to people she knew she would forget by tomorrow. There was some serious money here, Mara noted, as she noticed the stunning diamonds and pearls. A very attractive African/White American woman approached them with a knowing smile. She had honey-blond hair that fell in layers around her oval face and sparkling hazel eyes. She wore a beautiful gold dress that fell just past her knees. Gold sandals completed her outfit. Shari moved to meet her and the two hugged and kissed.

"Shari, it's so good to have you back. I've missed you." The woman smiled, taking Shari's hands, and looked her over. "You look absolutely beautiful," she commented.

"Thank you, Kate. It's good to be home," Shari told her. "I want you to meet someone." Shari turned to Mara, holding out her hand to her. Mara moved up to them.

"This is Mara Evans. Mara, Kate Rhone."

"Mara, I've heard a lot about you." Kate's smile was warm as she kissed her cheek. Mara was flattered by the warm welcome.

"I'm glad you could join us," Kate said.

"Thank you, and happy birthday."

"Thank you, dear, just don't ask me my age." Kate winked at her. Mara liked her instantly. Kate had made her feel welcome and she appreciated that.

An older white man approached them, then greeted Shari with a hug and kiss. Shari introduced him as Patrick Rhone Sr. He was over six feet, a little pudgy, with gray-brown hair and blue eyes. Mr. Rhone placed an arm about his wife, who gazed up at him lovingly. They made a great couple.

The party was great. Franklin kept close to Mara, engaging her in every dance that he could. She finally got away from him long enough to share a drink with Shari.

"Franklin's in love," Shari teased.

"Oh please, he's just a kid. How old is he, anyway?"

"Twenty-one."

She shrugged. "Just a kid, but he is cute." Mara smiled, sipping her wine. "I do like your future in-laws—they're very nice."

"Shari," a male voice called out. Mara turned to see a very handsome, dark Native American man coming toward them. He was tall, dark, and stunning to look at, almost too handsome. He wore two long braids over his shoulders. He was exotic for a man, she thought. His deep-set black eyes zoned in on Mara, holding her captive.

"Stone." Shari moved to greet him.

"Shari, it's good to see you. It's been a long time."

Stone looked right at Mara. He stared at her so openly that Mara felt a bit uncomfortable under his exploring gaze.

"Stone, I'd like you to meet Mara Evans. Mara, Stone Black," Shari introduced them. Stone instantly moved toward Mara, taking her hand. His eyes studied her face as if intrigued.

"It's a pleasure." Stone smiled, his eyes softening.

"Patrick!" Shari suddenly cried out.

Mara followed her gaze to see Patrick making his way toward them, his eyes fixed on Shari. Patrick was a handsome sight, at six feet, lean and muscular, with light brown hair and blue eyes. He looked like his father, only a little darker in color. He was handsomely dressed in a gray suit with a black shirt. Mara watched as he came to a stop in front of Shari, who was simply staring at him. Patrick bent to Shari and kissed her on the lips. Mara had never seen anything so romantic. He took Shari's hands and pulled her into his arms, then the two of them held each other. Mara looked around her to see that she wasn't the only one staring at them with admiration.

"I'll be over there somewhere," she whispered to them.

Patrick looked at her and smiled. "Hey, Mara, it's good see you," Patrick pulled her into his arms, giving her his usual bear hug. She returned his hug as he kissed her cheek. "Damn, girl, you look good."

"Thank you," she said and smiled back at him. She had always liked Patrick. He was amusing and open, a lot like her and the complete opposite of Shari, who was quiet and reserved. Their differences made them a great couple. Plus, they were hopelessly in love—anyone could see that.

Stone and Patrick exchanged greetings before Patrick turned back to Shari. He touched her face, gazing deeply into her eyes.

"Come with me," Stone whispered in her ear, taking her arm and leading her away from the loving couple. Stone got two fresh glasses and led her out into the garden. Mara sat on a bench and inhaled the fresh night air as it caressed her skin. She opened her eyes to find Stone staring intensely at her. Mara looked at him with caution.

"Should I be worried about you staring at me like that?"

He laughed, "No, no. Sorry for staring—your features are very captivating."

Mara smiled at his compliment, relaxing. "Thanks, but you know it's kind of weird, don't you?

"You have the most perfect, round features— your lips, your nose—just perfect."

"Thanks, I guess." She gazed at him cautiously.

"I've made you uncomfortable? I'm sorry. I'm an artist—you must let me draw you."

"What?" She was a bit surprised by his request.

"You have to let me sketch you." He studied her face even more.

"I'm sure there are much finer women you'd like to sketch."

"None with features like yours. Magnificent," he said, amazed. "I have a showing in a few days— would you come? I'm sure Shari will be there. You'll get to see my work—and perhaps see that I'm not a weird as you think."

"Artistic, not weird," she told him, and he laughed. "And, I'd love to come to your show."

He smiled, took her hand, and kissed it. "It will be a pleasure having you there."

"Great. I feel like dancing—join me?" He got up, holding a hand out to her. Mara followed him inside and they hit the dance floor. He could dance, and she found him engaging and delightful. After their third number, they took another garden break, cooling off with chilled wine.

"So what do you do?" Stone asked, sitting beside her.

"I just graduated from Howard."

"H.U. Congratulations."

"Thanks."

"So what will you be doing when you return to D.C.?"

"I have a degree in computer programming."

He looked at her, surprised. "Computers—it doesn't exactly suit your persona."

"How would you know?" she asked, amused.

"The way you move, the light in your eyes. I see an artist in you."

Mara stared at him, a bit taken aback by his revelation. "You see all that?"

"Oh, yeah." Stone was a free spirit with a real zest for life, and she enjoyed that about him.

"You might be right."

"So tell me," he insisted.

"I like to sketch."

"I knew it. What do you sketch?"

"Chairs, lately, but mostly accessories. Bags are my favorite."

"I knew it."

"They are just sketches, though."

"I'd love to see them."

"Maybe," she shrugged.

"Protective—that's good."

"It's not that, really, it's just that I don't like to show my sketches. It's a hobby, nothing more."

"From the look in your eyes, I'd say it's a lot more," Stone told her, cupping her chin in his hand and looking deeply into her eyes. Mara smiled at him, glad they shared a creative interest. He was the first person she had ever felt she could freely share her talent with, besides Shari, without risking ridicule. Mara had learned at an early age to hide her talent. Being a designer wasn't a good career, not for an urban Black girl who'd grown up watching her mother struggle the way she had. Mara had buried her talent, opting to merely sketch her ideas. Her mother knew of her talent, but was afraid it wasn't financially secure. Her mother didn't want to see her struggling the way she had and wanted a solid career for Mara, who also enjoyed computers, so she had concentrated on that.

"Stone." A familiar voice interrupted them. Mara looked up to see Zander. He was dressed in a charcoal-gray suit with a white mock-neck shirt underneath. He sure was a sexy man, even with his five o'clock shadow and that nasty frown on his face.

"Zander." Stone stood up and extended a hand to Zander, who shook it briefly.

"Could you excuse us?" Zander demanded. Stone looked at Mara, puzzled. Mara looked at Stone, not knowing what to say. Zander was dismissing Stone—they all knew that. It made Mara's blood boil, but she held her tongue.

"I will see you soon." Stone said to her.

"Of course," she replied and smiled at him. Stone dropped a kiss on her cheek before walking off.

"That was rude," she stated as soon as Stone was out of hearing distance. Zander's eyes narrowed with disapproval. What the hell was that about? she wondered.

"You really shouldn't encourage men you don't know." His tone was harsh, chilling. Mara cocked her head, looking at him. If she didn't know any better, she'd think he was being overprotective. But he couldn't be! His eyes went cold, and she knew he wasn't; he was just being rude.

"Have you seen my sister?"

"She's with her man."

"So Patrick is here?"

"That should please you."

He slowly looked her over, his eyes appraising her as he did. Mara felt her body warm under his gaze. Why was he looking at her like that? He had done it before, which left her wondering what he was thinking.

He was about to say something when a pretty blonde with striking green eyes came up behind him. She wrapped her arms around his waist and kissed his cheek. She was model-thin with large breasts that threatened to spill over the top of her designer dress. She was exactly the kind of woman Mara had pictured with a man like Zander. She was all glam.

Zander turned to the woman. A brief look of surprise crossed his face. The woman reached up and kissed him full on the lips, leaving a trace of shimmering red lipstick.

"Tanya?"

"Hello, darling," Tanya cooed seductively as she hugged him. Tanya pressed her body full into Zander, her mouth inches from his ear. "I missed you." The woman gave Mara a quick, disapproving once-over.

"Tanya, I thought you were in Paris," Zander said, pulling away. Tanya caressed his biceps.

"Paris got boring, so I'm home now." She kissed him again. He didn't return her kiss, but he didn't seem to mind her affections, either. "I just saw Shari. My guess is she's finally home." Tanya wiped her lipstick off Zander's cheek and lips.

"Yes, Shari's home," Zander responded.

"So, who's your little friend?" Tanya glared at her. It was obvious the woman didn't like her, although she didn't even know her. Then again, Mara really didn't care.

Zander's eyes came back to Mara. "This is Mara Evans—Mara, Tanya Steward. Mara and Shari went to Howard together."

"Oh, I see. I guess you're here for the wedding. How nice."

"Excuse me," Mara said and got up and started to walk away.

"How intuitive of her," Tanya said, and Mara turned, giving her a cold look before continuing on. No wonder Shari disliked her. She was a right-out bitch. Zander didn't even notice it. She was beautiful and obviously in love with Zander, or at least the idea of him.

Mara went in search of Stone, finding him by the

bar. They hit the dance floor. Mara intended to enjoy herself, and she did. She drank, she danced, she made polite conversation. All in all, it was a good night.

It was getting late, and Mara was tired. Plus, her feet hurt. She hadn't seen Shari for hours and wondered where she was.

"I can take you home," Stone offered as he walked her outside toward the parked cars where drivers waited. She searched the crowd for the one who had brought them to the party. She couldn't remember who he was.

"I came with Shari and I'd rather leave with her."

"I think Shari already left with Patrick."

"I think you're right," Mara sighed.

"Tell you what—why don't I go find your driver. Wait here."

"Thanks."

As Stone took off, she saw Zander coming toward her, minus Tanya. She rolled her eyes at him and turned away—she didn't care to deal with him and his rudeness right now. She was just too tired.

"Leaving?" he asked dryly.

She sighed wearily. "Yes, I'm tired." She didn't look at him, praying that Stone would show up.

"You can ride with me," Zander said. "My car is right here." He took her arm before she could protest and led her to his Lincoln Town Car. His driver, a thick Italian-American, opened the door for them as Zander assisted her into the car. Mara was too tired even to protest. She sank into the seat, grateful to be off her feet, then slipped off her shoes as Zander got in beside her. His cologne invaded her senses. She closed her eyes, trying to block him out, but she was too aware of him. He had a fiancée—plus, she really didn't like him too much.

They drove in silence for a while, which Mara appreciated as she flexed her tired feet. She could feel him looking at her. She shifted to meet his piercing eyes, though his gaze revealed nothing.

"What happened to your girlfriend? No reunion tonight?"

"Why your sudden interest?"

"Trust me—I'm not," she threw back at him. She closed her eyes, leaning her head back against the headrest to block out the sight of him. His life was none of her business. She'd told herself she wouldn't get involved, and it was best she kept it that way.

Zander watched Mara as she pretended to sleep. Something had lured him to the Rhones' party tonight. He hadn't planned on attending, but he hadn't been able to stop thinking of her. He liked and respected Stone, but he didn't like the idea of Mara having a relationship with him.

Quietly, he admired Mara's petite but curvaceous figure in the black dress; her legs were magnificent and she had beautiful feet. Tanya had been gone for two months, yet seeing her tonight had only annoyed him. All he could think of was Mara. She was the reason he had gone to the Rhones' party. What was it about this woman? Somehow just being near her pleased him.

* * *

Mara awoke as something gently caressed her cheek. She opened her eyes to see Zander. He smiled at her and she sat up, realizing they were at the house.

"Want me to carry you in?" He grinned. She wanted to smack the grin off his face.

"I can walk," she said, and reached for her shoes. He got to them first and handed them to her. She took them and put them on. He got out first and held his hand out to assist her. She paused for a second, and then placed her hand into his. His hand was strong and solid as he helped her from the car. As she straightened up, she lost her footing and stumbled right into him. His arms instantly went around her waist to steady her. As he pulled her against him, her body reacted to the closeness and his touch. She quickly pushed away from him and steadied her footing.

She glanced at him as his eyes held hers. He had a woman. She quickly walked away, heading up the stairs to the front door. He moved quickly past her to open the door for her. He was still too close. What the hell was he up to?

"Thanks." She brushed past him as she went inside.

"You're welcome," he whispered and shivers raced down her spine, causing her nipples to harden.

"Good night," she quickly told him, not looking back as she climbed the stairs. Her heart was racing with thoughts that she needed to keep under control. He was off limits. He was engaged.

"Good night," he responded in a deep, sexy voice. She trembled at his tone, but kept going.

What was wrong with her? Why was he affecting her so much? She didn't even like him. She couldn't like him.

In her room, Mara stripped down, cleaned her face, and fell into bed. Her body still tingled from being so close to him. What was happening to her? She wasn't supposed to feel this way, not about Zander Tuskcan, of all people. She moaned and turned over onto her back. It was hopeless.

Chapter 7

It was almost two in the morning, and Zander couldn't sleep. Images of Mara kept haunting him. He had to admit she had filled out that dress nicely tonight with her thick thighs and nicely rounded behind. He recalled her softness as she fell onto him, and he wanted to feel her against him again. Naked, preferably. Cursing his primal need for her, he got out of bed and took a cold shower. He felt a little better, but it didn't quite quench the urge surging in him.

Zander pulled on a pair of silk pj bottoms and tossed a towel around his neck to catch the water from his hair and headed downstairs. He entered the kitchen and stopped dead in his tracks. There she was—the woman who had kept him awake into the morning. Obviously, sleep had also eluded her, and he wondered why. As she reached for a glass on tiptoe, the short cotton nightgown moved up, revealing those strong, brown thighs and that very nice rear. She wore blue panties this time. She grabbed the glass and dropped back onto her heels, closing the door, then turned and saw him. She gasped and dropped the glass. He watched as it shattered around her bare feet.

"Oh, damn!" As she started to move, he saw the pieces of sharp glass around her bare feet.

"Don't!" He held a hand up, stopping her. She remained still. "You might get cut," he warned. "Let me get that—just don't move."

He grabbed the Dustbuster off the wall and proceeded to vacuum up the bits of glass around her feet. He noticed the toe ring—very sexy. His eyes traveled the length of her legs to stop at the edge of her nightgown. She had great legs for a short woman.

He finished vacuuming and stood back, looking at her.

"Thank you. But you really shouldn't sneak up on me like that."

"Did I?" He rose to his full height, looking down at her. He hadn't meant to frighten her.

"I guess you're not used to someone being around." She cocked her head, studying him. He watched as her eyes slowly drifted down to his chest.

"I guess." He wondered what she was thinking. Was she attracted to him, the way he was to her? He suddenly wanted to know. He saw a ting of desire in her eyes as she looked at his naked upper body. She was attracted to him. He felt himself harden and was thankful his baggy pj's hid his true thoughts. Water dripped down the side of his face and he used the end of the towel to dry it. He watched her watch his every move with interest, her eyes lingering on his chest. Once again he came under her open stare. She suddenly blinked and shook her head, then looked into his eyes. All evidence of desire was gone from her eyes; he was disappointed.

She moved and cried out, lifting her right foot. A

few drops of blood fell onto the white tile as he quickly picked her up. She gasped in surprise at his sudden movement. She grabbed onto his neck, her lips mere inches from his. Her warm breath tickled his neck. He took her over to the dining table and sat her down in one of the chairs.

He got a piece of napkin and returned to her, taking hold of her foot and placing it under her heel.

"Hold it!" he told her.

She crossed her legs, cradling her injured foot. He caught a glimpse of her panties, then moved away to gather his thoughts and clean up the few drops of blood off the floor. His attraction to her was growing, and it scared and excited him at the same time. He finished by washing his hands and turned to her. She looked up at him with those big, brown eyes, biting her bottom lip. He took a deep breath and stilled his body against the surge of desire that ignited deep within him. What was she doing to him? He refocused his thoughts.

"Can you feel the glass?" he asked, kneeling before her to inspect her foot. He could see the tiny bit of glass embedded in her heel. It needed to come out.

"I have to take you upstairs and get it out." As he picked her up again, she wrapped her arms around his neck and held on. He stilled his body against her closeness, but he couldn't deny the fact that she felt good in his arms.

Mara fought the urge to bury her face in Zander's neck and inhale his fresh scent. His wet hair

dripped down his shoulders, soaking her nightgown. His skin was warm to the touch as he carried
her upstairs into his private bathroom. She barely
caught a glimpse of his king-size sledge bed.
Thoughts of them making love in the bed flashed
before her. Stop it!

His bathroom was twice the size of hers, with a
separate tub/Jacuzzi and a glass-enclosed shower.
There were two sinks, one across from the other.
She felt a chill against her right breast and looked
down to see that his wet hair had soaked her nightgown, causing it to stick to her breast. She watched
his powerful back muscle flex as he reached for
something in the chest. He turned and his eyes fell
on her damp nightgown, and her nipples hardened. She let out a gentle breath as his eyes
lingered on her breasts. She prayed that they'd lose
their hardness. It was hopeless with him looking at
her the way he was.

She watched him as he knelt in front of her and
took hold of her foot, his hand warm against her
leg. Her nightgown fell back, revealing her panties.
She had no time to pull her gown down as she had
to grip the side of the tub so she wouldn't fall in.
His hands were gentle as he used tweezers to pull
the small piece of glass from the heel of her foot,
then clean the cut with alcohol.

"There. You should live now," he said jokingly.
Mara got up and quickly pulled down her nightgown. She caught their reflection in the mirror. He
was half-naked and she was in a damp nightgown.
As he turned to the sink, their eyes met in the mirror, and he lowered his head and started to wash his

hands. The sexual tension between them was off the charts.

"Thank you, and sorry I broke the glass." She studied him from the back, wanting to run her fingers down his spine, feel the smooth warmness of his flesh again. Having him half-naked in front of her was not helping. She swallowed her desire.

"Don't worry about it. I'm just glad you weren't cut any worse." She grabbed a towel and handed it to him. He took it and wiped his hand.

"Thanks." He pushed his hair back from his face. He had such nice hair, she thought.

Mara reached out and fingered his hair; it was silky to the touch. She heard his sharp intake of breath and looked into his eyes.

"It's tangling up," she said. "Sit down and let me help you dry it." She pulled down the toilet seat lid and he sat, no objections. She took the same towel he had used to dry his hands and began to towel-dry his hair. After she massaged his scalp, she reached for a comb and started to section his hair to gently comb out the tangles.

"You do that well," he commented in a soothing voice.

His hair was wonderful. She liked long hair, just not on herself, of course. It was too hard to maintain with hair as thick as hers.

"I had a job shampooing hair at a salon."

"What else have you done besides hair?" She continued to comb through his hair, enjoying the rich texture of it.

"You name it, I've done it, but hair was my all-time favorite. I loved doing hair. Once you get your fingers into someone's scalp, their whole life is an open book." She ran her fingers through the untangled area of his hair, pushing it to one side, and started working on the other side.

"So what did you study at Howard?"

"Shari didn't tell you?"

"No."

"I've been friends with Shari for four years now, and you mean to tell me she never once told you about me?"

"Shari and I don't exactly talk much."

"I studied computer technology," she said.

"Computers. Good choice."

"Yeah, my mother thought so, too."

"You don't like computers?"

"It's not my first love."

"Which is?"

"I wanted to be a designer."

"Doesn't sound so bad. What kind of designs?"

"I started off with clothes and accessories, but the last year I've been getting into chairs."

"Chairs?" He sounded surprised.

"Yeah, you know those kinds of chairs you find in restaurants and hotels? Tables are easy, but chairs? The right one can say a lot." She massaged his scalp, thinking of her chairs and how much pleasure she got out of creating a new design. When she heard Zander moan, she stopped, realizing she was massaging him a bit too much.

"Have you ever made one of your chairs?"

"No, but I did reupholster our kitchen chairs last summer. My mother was very impressed. She showed them to all her friends." Mara smiled, recalling the many compliments she'd received about the chairs.

"Why didn't you study design?"

"I had to make sure I could take care of my mother once I got out of college. She's worked far too long and hard to be cleaning floors all her life. Once I get back to D.C. and find a job that can support both of us, she's retiring."

"Sounds like a plan."

"One can't exactly make it without one."

"I'd like to see your designs if you have any with you." He was the second man who had asked to see her designs. No one except her mother and Shari had ever seen her sketches, but now both Stone and Zander wanted to see her work. It was flattering.

"OK. There. Done," she told him and stepped back. He got up and looked in the mirror, running his fingers through his hair.

"Thank you." He smiled down at her.

She stared at his lips, wondering what they would taste like. She had to get away from him. Right now.

"Well, good night." She cleared her throat and moved toward the door. Suddenly he grabbed her arm, stopping her. She turned and looked at him and before she knew it, he pulled her to him and his mouth came down on hers, hard and hungry. A shiver raced like wildfire through her body, but Tanya's face flashed before her and she pushed him away, angry.

"What the hell are you doing?" She demanded, managing to find her voice.

"I'm sorry—I shouldn't have done that." He raked his fingers through his hair. "I thought you wanted me to." He ran his hand over his face, letting out a deep breath.

"To what?" she asked, unable to hide her anger.

He didn't answer, just stared at her. What the hell was his game? He was engaged. How the hell could he kiss her like that?

"I'm sorry, I just assumed . . ."

"Don't assume anything about me!" she cut him off, and stormed out.

She was boiling mad. How could he kiss her when he had a fiancée? Granted, there was that attraction thing between them, but that gave him no right. And him assuming that she wanted him to—that just did it! She was mad—mad at herself mostly, for wanting him. She stomped up the stairs, fuming. She had wanted that kiss and he had given it. But it still didn't change the fact that he was engaged.

Chapter 8

Mara sat by the pool over a late breakfast, trying not to think of the kiss. She really had to be careful with him. She couldn't let him pull her into something she knew she would regret. She would be back in D.C. in less than a month. She did not need to get involved with Zander—it would be crazy. They were nowhere near compatible—plus, he was way out of her league.

Shari joined her with a gleam in her eyes.

"So I guess the reunion went well?" Mara teased, and Shari blushed.

"It did." Shari sat across from her and started munching on some fruit.

"How did you get home? The limousine was still at the house," Shari asked as she poured herself a cup of coffee. Mara passed her the sugar.

"I got a ride with Zander."

"Zander was there?" Shari asked, surprised as she added cream to her coffee.

"Yep, and so was Tanya. Didn't you see her?"

"No, I, ah, left with Patrick soon after he got there."

Shari was hopelessly in love with Patrick, but it was a good thing. Mara was very happy for her.

"So, was my brother pleasant?"

"As pleasant as he gets," Mara answered dryly.

"What happened?"

"Nothing. I fell asleep during the ride back," Mara told her in a hurry, and Shari looked at her suspiciously.

"Oh, I see." Shari eyed her.

Zander kissing her would remain a secret. Shari was her best friend and she told her everything, but this one was a no-no.

"You were hoping for more?"

"Good morning," his unmistakable voice said behind them, and Mara felt her stomach do a flip. How could one man have such an intense effect on her in such a short time? She looked up at him as he approached the table. He was dressed in a dark blue suit with a white shirt and burgundy tie. She watched as he dropped a kiss on his sister's cheek before taking a seat. He poured himself some coffee, adding only sugar, then took a sip. His lips seemed as if they were caressing the edge of the cup. Mara swallowed hard as she recalled the feel of those lips on hers. She blinked and looked away.

"You're not going to be late?" Shari asked, a hint of surprise in her voice.

"No. So how are things going with Patrick?"

Shari frowned, then responded, not too kindly, "I'm not going to run away again, so you can stop worrying."

"That's not what I asked."

Shari sulked, sinking into her chair. Mara watched them closely, noting the tension between them.

"We're fine."

"Good." He looked at Mara and she felt her heart race. The kiss flashed in her mind. She looked away, sipping her coffee. She had to control her emotions.

"Slept well?" He had a knowing smirk on his face that annoyed Mara.

She licked her lips, then calmly answered, "Yes, thanks."

"Good. I'd like both of you to join me for dinner later. I'll send a car around seven," he told them.

"Dinner sounds nice." He looked at her with an intense stare and she went warm beneath his gaze.

"I'll see you both later, then," he said, getting up and leaving. Mara watched him walk away, liking the way he moved with such confidence and sexuality. Tanya was a lucky woman.

"I can't believe he just did that," Shari exclaimed with skepticism.

"What? What did he do?"

"Zander never has time for dinner, except with his business partners."

"Really?"

"Really," Shari nodded.

Zander had to cancel a late meeting to have dinner with Shari and Mara. He knew he shouldn't have done it, but he wanted to see Mara. He found her delightful, and the fact that he didn't intimidate her turned him on. He couldn't stop thinking about her. He knew he shouldn't have kissed her the way he did, but having her that close had affected him in ways he never thought possible. Zander was used to women throwing themselves at him, but he knew Mara wouldn't. She was strong and she knew who she was. The intense attraction he felt toward her was different for a man like him.

His thoughts drifted to Tanya. He had known her for over seven years now. He did business with her family. That was how he had met her, at a business dinner with her father. He had always thought she was a beautiful woman and would make a good wife. Tanya was familiar and she fit right into his lifestyle, unlike Mara, who was so not his style.

Zander was running late. By the time he had gotten to the restaurant, Shari and Mara had already finished their appetizers. Zander offered his apologies.

Mara was dressed in a powder-blue sweater and black slacks. She wore gold stud earrings. He noted her bare neck and wrist. She needed more jewelry to complement her look. Her short hair was brushed back from her face, her brown skin glowing in the soft light of the restaurant. Her sparkling, dark-brown eyes assessed him openly. He liked the way she looked at him, as if he was naked. It was sensual.

"We almost gave up on you," she said with a smile.

He wanted to kiss her. "I'm glad you didn't," he said. "So what have you two ordered?"

"Nothing yet." Shari picked up her menu.

Zander picked up his menu and flipped right to the dinner section, his appetite coming back.

Mara was enjoying her roast duck dinner and chatting along with Shari and Zander. It was nice to see them communicating without fighting. Zander was warm and funny and totally at ease.

"So what about you?" he asked and Mara looked at him, puzzled. She had been thinking so hard about him that she had zoned out in the middle of the conversation.

"What about me?"

"Plan on getting married one day?" The question threw her. She stared at him for a few seconds before responding.

"Yes. When are you?"

"Answer my question first," he said.

"Yes, answer the question," Shari chimed in.

Mara rolled her eyes at her. "I need a man for that, don't you think?"

"So you do plan on settling down?"

"When I find a decent man."

"Looking for Mr. Perfect?" Zander asked in a dry tone.

"There's no such thing as a perfect man or woman. If you can find someone whom you get along with, respect, love, and have good sex with, you're damn lucky."

He stared at her, intrigued, while Shari tried not to laugh.

"What?" Mara asked innocently as he continued to stare at her.

Zander sipped his wine, his eyes fixed on her.

"Zander, darling," a female voice called out. Mara looked to see Tanya coming toward them. She was stunning in a red cocktail dress. Her blond hair was in big, soft curls. Again, Mara found herself wondering why Zander had kissed her when he had his model. Zander got up to greet her with a hug and a light kiss.

"What are you doing here?" Tanya asked, caressing Zander's cheek, oblivious to anyone else.

"I'm having dinner with my sister and Mara. You remember Mara, don't you?" Zander gestured toward Tanya and she turned her cold green eyes on Mara. The woman definitely didn't like her.

"Yes, nice to see you again, Mar."

"It's Mara, M-a-r-a." She spelled her name out, knowing it would annoy Tanya.

"Right." Tanya turned her attention to Shari and gave her a bright smile. "Hi, Shari. We have to do lunch sometime."

"Maybe after the wedding. I'm kind of busy—you understand."

"Yes, of course."

"Who are you here with?" Zander asked.

"My brother. Why don't you join us?"

"I'm with Shari and Mara right now," Zander said, annoyed.

"I'm sure they won't mind." Tanya smiled at Shari, who forced a dry smile.

"I'll call you tomorrow," Zander said curtly and kissed Tanya's cheek. She sighed in frustration and stormed off.

"What's her problem?" Mara asked as Zander sat down.

"Let me apologize for that," Zander started.

"Why should you? She was the one who was rude," Shari objected.

"She usually doesn't act like that." Zander tried to convince her, but Mara knew better.

A silent tension fell at the table. It was obvious Tanya's presence had spoiled the evening.

"So now do you see what I was saying about Zander with her?" Shari roared as she followed Mara into her room. The minute they had gotten to the house, Zander had headed to his library, claiming he had work to do.

"Maybe he likes his women that way," Mara said as she plopped in the armchair and slipped off her shoes.

"She doesn't love him. You have to help me out here," Shari pleaded, but Mara really didn't want to get involved.

"And you want me to tell him that his woman isn't right for him?"

"Exactly."

"And how am I supposed to do that?"

"Talk him out of making a mistake."

"You're his sister, I'm just a guest. I don't think that is my responsibility."

Shari looked defeated. "You're right, I'm sorry. I shouldn't have asked you to do such a thing. I just hate seeing him with her, especially when I know what she's about."

Mara understood Shari's need but she couldn't get involved in their lives. Not like that.

In her room Mara cleaned her face and changed her clothes, putting on a long T-shirt with Minnie Mouse on the front of it. She ventured into Shari's room to find her hanging up the phone. Shari didn't look too happy.

Mara sat beside her on the bed. "What's wrong?"

"Patrick's off to Atlanta again."

"When's he coming back?"

"Three days."

"Just three days?" she asked, surprised. "So what's the problem?"

"I think he has a mistress."

"What? Why would you think that?" Mara stuttered.

"I don't know. It's just a feeling."

"And how long have you had this feeling?"

"A while now, especially since he goes to Atlanta so much."

"Have you asked him?"

"I can't. I'm too scared and I don't think I want to know."

"Yes, you do. I know you."

"Oh God, Mara, what should I do?" Shari leaned her head on Mara's shoulders and put her arms around her friend.

"What makes you think he's cheating on you?"

"Because I cheated on him." She moaned.

Mara was shocked. She got up and looked down at Shari.

"It was a one-night stand."

Mara placed her hands on her hips and glared at her. She couldn't believe Shari had had a one-night stand.

"You were sick that weekend."

"Does Patrick know about this one-night stand?"

"No."

"So because of that, you think he cheated on you?"

"Yes."

Mara couldn't help but laugh. "Girl, please—it's just guilt that's messing with your head."

"Do you think I should tell Patrick?"

"Hell, no. I say, let it stay buried."

"I don't know, Mara."

"Tell you what. If he comes clean to you about another woman, then you do the same. But I wouldn't tell him. While a woman will readily forgive a man, he won't do the same with her. Trust me on this one."

Shari looked torn, and Mara knew she was going to tell him regardless. She prayed it wouldn't ruin their marriage.

Back in her room, Mara called her mother.

"So how de' vacation goin'?"

Mara smiled as she cradled the phone at her ear in bed. "It's going good and interesting, especially with Zander's girlfriend," Mara said.

Mara told her mother the whole story, except for her attraction toward Zander and the kiss.

"Yu' jus' be careful an' don't get too involved. I know Shari is yu' friend but be careful with other people's family matters."

"I know. So how was Baltimore Harbor?"

"It was nice, real nice."

"Listen, Mama, I don't want you to feel alone, so if you want me to come home, I will."

"No, I don't want yu' to come home. I want yu' to stay an' enjoy yu'self. Yu' enjoyin' yu'self, right?"

"Yes, I am," Mara admitted.

"Good, so yu' can stop worrin' 'bout me."

"OK, good night."

"'Night, baby."

She was glad her mother was having some fun in life, especially knowing how hard she worked.

Mara headed downstairs for some warm milk. She was on her way out of the kitchen when she ran into Zander coming out of his library. He had removed his jacket. His shirt was out of his pants and half-unbuttoned and she could see a white tank beneath his shirt.

"'Night," she said when she realized she was staring. She started to walk away.

"Mara, wait." She stopped and gave him her attention. "I'd like to talk to you."

"About what?"

"The kiss."

It was something she had tried to forget. She frowned at him, wondering what he was up to.

"It's forgotten, so don't worry about it," she said.

"I can't forget it. I've tried, but I enjoyed it and I'm sure you did, too," he said with a confidence that warmed her.

"That's presumptuous of you." She was intrigued, which was not good. She had to be careful around him. He was a bit too intoxicating.

"Are you saying my kiss didn't affect you?"

"Can't say it did."

"I don't believe you."

"Like I care what you believe. You have a woman, in case you forgot," she reminded him.

"Tanya and I have an understanding."

"Really? And what kind of understanding is that?"

"She understands our situation."

"And what situation is that?"

He looked frustrated for a brief moment. "Damn, you ask a lot of questions."

"I can play dumb if you like," she whispered in a sexy voice while she batted her lashes. He threw back his head and laughed. He stopped laughing and looked at her seriously, studying her as she sipped her milk. He stepped towards her and she felt her heart race.

"Are you for real?" She held up a hand.

He stopped in his tracks. "I don't understand the question."

"You have a woman and yet you stand there telling me how much you want to kiss me? What the hell kind of man are you?"

She rolled her eyes at him and walked away. She was mad. Mad at him for wanting to kiss her when he had a woman, and the fact that she wanted him to. She had to be careful from now on, real careful.

Chapter 9

Mara was taking notes from Helen on how to make her special three-fruit pie when Shari walked into the kitchen, looking disappointed.

"What's up?"

Shari flopped down on a stool nearby.

"Patrick and I were supposed to go to this art show tonight, but of course, he's in Atlanta. I really don't want to miss this show."

"I'll go with you."

"Would you?"

"It's Stone's show, right?"

Shari looked at her, surprised. "Yes. How did you know?"

"He told me."

"When did you meet Stone?"

"Kate's party—you introduced us just as Patrick showed up."

Shari blushed. "Oh. I really need to buy a few pieces for our new house."

"New house?" She'd never heard Shari talk about a house before. Then again, she and Patrick were getting married.

"Patrick is having one built for us. It's not far from here—about five miles, actually. He's been

working on it for two years. It's going to take another year before our house is ready. You definitely
have to come back for the housewarming party."

"I wouldn't miss it."

Mara was dressed in a lavender short skirt suit
that showed off her legs. The jacket had a plunging
neckline and one button in the middle. Under it
she wore a sheer black tank. She also wore heels
that were a bit too high for her taste, but they did
wonders for her legs. Shari wore a blue silk wrap
dress that showed off her long, lean figure.

The gallery was located in downtown Spring Lake,
in an old warehouse with bare walls and hardwood
floors. People milled about, taking in the magnificent art on the walls. Mara was impressed by Stone's
work. She especially loved the way he played with colors to capture the little details of his subjects. Most of
the artist's work depicted landscapes and there were
a few with Native American themes. But she was
mostly impressed with the array of breathtaking ab-
stract pieces. Mara spent almost half an hour staring
at a piece with a single horse drinking from a lake.
She loved the way Stone had captured the details of
the land and the horse blending into one with the
backdrop of the setting sun.

"Beautiful, isn't it?" Shari came up to her. Mara
couldn't stop staring at the painting.

"Yeah, it is."

"Thank God I was able to buy it."

"You did?"

Shari grinned happily. "I figured it was a good
buy from the way it captivated you."

"It does. I love it. This guy is very talented."

"Ladies," a male voice exclaimed behind them. Mara turned to see Stone, who was dressed all in gray, his two long braids hanging over his shoulders. He wore turquoise jewelry. He looked at Mara, his eyes searching her face.

"Stone," Shari said and embraced him, kissing his cheeks.

"Mara." He smiled at her.

Mara smiled at him.

"Thanks for coming." Stone looked at Shari.

"I wouldn't miss it for the world. You know how much I love your work," Shari said.

"Thank you, love." He looked at Mara again.

"Your work is amazing. Congratulations," Mara told him.

"Thank you."

"Excuse me, I see an old friend," Shari said, and left them alone.

Stone moved closer to Mara, his eyes holding her captive. He reached up and caressed her bottom lip with his thumb.

"Beautiful," he whispered. Mara stepped back, a bit uncomfortable with his openness.

"You have to let me sketch you," he told her, looking her over slowly. He then ran his hand down her arm.

"Could you tone it down?" she asked, when she noticed a few people staring at them.

"Sorry. You inspire me."

"Come, let me show you my work," he said, holding out an arm to her. She smiled and took it. He took her about the room, explaining his works to her. Stone would stop briefly and introduce her to his friends and colleges. Mara was having such a great time that she simply played along. She liked Stone's spirit and his delightful eccentricity. He fascinated her.

"Can I ask you something?" he said as he handed her a fresh glass of white wine. They stepped out into the garden patio of the gallery to get some air. The cool evening breeze was welcoming.

"Sure."

"Would it be too soon to ask you out? I mean, in the little time I've spent with you, I feel like I've known you forever." He smiled sweetly at her. "Lunch, maybe?" His eyes pleaded with her. She knew she couldn't tell him no. What harm would lunch with him do anyway?

"I'd like that."

He looked relieved and happy. "Thank you."

"Are you sure?" Shari asked her for the tenth time on their way home.

"Is there something about Stone I should know? You'd better tell me now."

"No, Stone is a nice man. I just can't see the two of you together, that's all."

"Why not? He's an artist and actually inspires me." She saw Shari frown. "It's only lunch. It's not as if I'm going to sleep with him."

"Would you?"

"Girl, please, what is your problem? You know I don't sleep with just anyone. I just met the man, and he asked me to lunch. It's all innocent."

"What if he's attracted to you?"

"I think he already is. He did ask me out."

"But you're not attracted to him. So why go out with him?"

"Because he's interesting and I like him."

"Stone can be very seductive."

"I know."

"And you like that."

"I find him interesting—I'm not going to marry the man, so relax."

"He wants more than friendship," Shari said. "I'm telling you that right now."

"I know, Mother," Mara teased. "Come on. Lighten up—it's just lunch with a new friend."

"OK, fine."

Shari pouted, and Mara wondered why she was getting so bent out of shape about Stone. She wasn't attracted to Stone—plus, she was on vacation. She wasn't about to get involved with anyone here.

Chapter 10

Mara wore a violet halter dress and high-heeled mules for her lunch with Stone. He picked her up at the mansion in his BMW, wearing slacks and a mustard-colored dress shirt. He looked good. His hair was in one braid hanging down his back.

The restaurant was small and intimate, decorated with a modern theme. Mara learned that Stone had grown up poor on a reservation in Southampton, Long Island. His father had died when he was only ten, and his mother a year later of a broken heart. His only uncle, a lawyer based in Newark, had taken him in and raised him. Like most people, Stone was looking for the right woman. He had a five-year-old daughter named Amee with his high-school sweetheart. His daughter lived in Queens with her mother and stepfather. He saw his daughter every other weekend.

After lunch they went to a cafe. It was a nice day, so they sat outside. Mara sipped her cappuccino as she watched people go about their business.

"So what about you—how long will you be in New Jersey?" Stone asked.

"Just until Shari gets married—then I go back to D.C."

"And you don't have a boyfriend?"

"No." She smiled.

"Interesting—as attractive as you are, and no man."

"It's more like attracting the right man that's the problem."

"I know what you mean. It's hard to find that someone who complements you."

Mara could feel eyes boring into her and looked up to find Zander staring right at her. He was standing across the street at his car, his driver holding the door open for him. She smiled and was about to wave at him when he got into his car. Puzzled, Mara turned her attention back to Stone.

"Wasn't that Zander?" Stone said.

"Yeah, that was him," she said.

"I don't think he realized it was you."

"He did."

"He didn't look too pleased about seeing us together."

"Does Zander strike you as a man that's ever pleased about anything?" she asked, and Stone laughed.

"You are a delight," he said, and Mara recalled Zander telling her the same thing. She changed the subject and got Stone back to talking about his art.

By the time he dropped her off at the mansion it was almost dinnertime.

"Come to my studio tomorrow?" he asked as he walked her to the door.

"Why?"

"I need to sketch you."

"I don't think so."

"Please."

"No."

"I promise you won't regret it."

Mara cocked a curious brow at him. "You sure about that?"

"Promise."

"OK." She gave in with a smile. There wasn't any harm in him sketching her. She had seen some of his magnificent sketches.

"I'll sit for you, as long as you don't try to take it any further."

"I had a feeling you were going to say that." He looked briefly disappointed. "But I'll take whatever you are willing to give. I do enjoy your company."

"And I yours," she said.

"Friends, then?"

"Definitely."

"So how was it?" Shari asked the minute Mara entered her bedroom.

"It was very nice."

"So you'll be seeing him again?" Shari asked, suspicious.

"He wants to sketch me."

"Oh?" Shari seemed surprised.

"Something wrong with that?"

"No," Shari mumbled.

"Good. So what's going on with you?"

"I just don't see you with Stone."

"Really?"

"He's not for you."

"How would you know that?"

"Trust me."

Mara studied her friend, wondering why she was being negative toward Stone. Stone was cool and she liked him.

"I swear you and your brother are tripping."

"Zander? What did he do?"

"He saw me with Stone today."

"He did?"

"Yeah, and he ignored me, which I thought was very rude."

"Maybe he didn't want to disturb your *date*."

Mara hadn't thought of that. Maybe that was it and if it was, she still thought he was rude not to acknowledge her.

"Regardless of that fact, he didn't have to ignore me."

Shari got quiet. Mara looked at her, concerned. This had nothing to do with Stone. Something else was going on with Shari.

"Are you OK?"

"Patrick's coming home tonight," she said.

"And you are not happy?"

"I have to tell him, Mara. It's eating me."

"And before you do that, are you going to find out if he has another woman or not?" Mara asked her. Shari looked at her, perplexed. "Cover your behind first. That's all I'm saying."

Later that evening Shari left for Patrick's condo. Helen was spending the night with her daughter Kayla and her six-month-old grandson Jay, so Mara was alone. She put the radio on a classic soul station and started to make a light dinner of shrimp and pasta. She had just finished tossing the pasta and shrimp when Zander walked into the kitchen. They stared at each other.

"Where's Helen?" he finally spoke.

"Hello to you, too."

"Hello," he grunted.

"That's better," she said. "Helen is with her daughter."

"Oh." He looked around as if lost. His eyes then came to rest on the food she was preparing.

"I made enough for two. Care to join me?"

"Thank you," he said, discarding his jacket and case at the dining table.

Mara got two dinner plates and scooped the pasta onto them. Zander moved to the wine cooler unit and pulled out a bottle of white wine, uncorked it, and got two glasses. While she placed the plates on the dining table, he poured the wine. They did all this in silence.

"This is good," he said between bites.

"Thank you." She smiled at his compliment.

"So how was your lunch?" His eyes met and held hers, almost daring her to lie. Mara took a sip of her wine, never breaking eye contact, wondering about his interest. He had a woman.

"Lunch was wonderful and so was the company." She watched him closely. His eyes revealed nothing. "Were you expecting me to say it was horrible?"

"So you like him?"

"Yeah, he's interesting."

"Interesting?" Zander mused. She wondered what he was thinking. "So you will be seeing him again?"

"Why?"

"You should be careful with him."

"Is he a rapist?"

"No."

"A serial killer?"

"No," he responded calmly.

"So what's the problem then?"

"I don't really care who you go out with. However, you are a guest, and I don't think you should get into anything you aren't prepared for."

Mara stared at him in wonder. Did she hear him right? Was he really giving her advice about men? She didn't get him. Talk about mixed signals. One minute he was all cold, the next he was being protective. Mara didn't know what to make of him.

"You have a fiancée, yet you keep coming on to me, wanting to kiss me. Now, who should I be more cautious of, you or Stone?" Mara waited for him to answer. When he didn't, she smiled with satisfaction.

"I guess it's none of my business," he responded calmly.

"Thanks for the heads-up, but I can take care of myself."

"I figured that," he said and finished his wine.

Mara got up and picked up the empty plates and took them into the kitchen. He brushed against her as he placed the wineglasses in the sink. Mara tried to ignore his closeness.

"Why don't you put those in the dishwasher?"

"It's only a few dishes," she said and started to wash them. He stood with his back to the edge of the counter and watched her. She looked outside at the pool. Night had fallen and a cool breeze floated through the windows, bringing in the scent of flowers from the garden. A soft rain had started to fall, and she could see the ripples reflecting off the pool's surface. She finished the dishes and he handed her a towel. She dried her hands.

"OK, what is it?" she asked, turning to him. His black, questioning eyes studied her.

"You have the most beautiful lips."

"Here we go again." She shook her head. "Why are you trying to seduce me?"

"I don't try," he said, his tone overflowing with seduction, "I do." He looked at her breasts. She knew he could see her hardened nipples. She wished her body didn't react to him so easily.

"When was the last time you made love to Tanya?"

His eyes returned to hers instantly. "Why?"

How could he be so cold? "Do you even love her?"

"She loves me," he said with ease.

She wondered what kind of relationship they really had. "Do you love her?"

"Like I said, we have an understanding."

"I'm gonna take that as a no." Mara shook her head, disappointed.

"I was in love once and it ended badly. I don't care to venture down that path again."

"So Tanya's just the means of obtaining your legacy?"

"Nicely put. But if you must know, I don't believe in love."

"Sounds like commitment issues to me."

"I guess you believe in love?"

"Yes, I do. Granted that it takes some of us a long time to find the real thing."

"I'd like to kiss you now," he said seductively. If only he wasn't so fine and so tempting, but she wasn't about to fall into his seductive trap. She would remain strong, God help her.

"You want me to be careful while I'm here, remember? So I'm being careful with you. So you can forget it." She walked away before he could respond. His rich laughter filled the room. Mara couldn't help the smile that touched her lips.

Mara was halfway up the stairs when the doorbell rang. She stopped and started to turn back when Zander entered the foyer and headed for the door. Zander gazed up at her with mischief in his eyes before he opened the door and Tanya entered.

"Darling!" Tanya cooed and wrapped herself around Zander. She wore all black, which made her appear even thinner than she was. She gave Zander a passionate kiss. Mara stilled her heart at the sight.

"Mmmm." Tanya stepped back, wiping her lipstick from his lips. He seemed uncomfortable with Tanya fussing over him.

"Darling, I've been calling you all evening," she cooed seductively to Zander. Tanya saw Mara then and stared at her with cold, hate-filled eyes. Mara shook her head and continued upstairs. She heard Zander telling Tanya to follow him into his library. Why did she have to be attracted to the one man who wasn't available—and out of her league? The thought of them together burned her deeply.

The minute Zander closed the door to his library, Tanya was on him, kissing him and rubbing his crotch. He suddenly found her advances annoying.

He gently eased her away from him. She wasn't exactly the woman he wanted to kiss at the moment. Full, round lips flashed before his eyes. He blinked and focused on Tanya.

"What's wrong? It's been a while, Zander. You dismissed me at the restaurant and that hurt. What's going on? Is there something I should know?" Tanya's green eyes searched his. He knew he couldn't do it anymore.

"No, I'm just tired," he lied.

"I should have called."

"Why don't we have dinner tomorrow night?"

"My place?"

"Sounds good."

He smiled at her. She quickly moved up to him and kissed him deeply. He eased her away from him; he just couldn't respond to her.

"So tomorrow, then," he said as he led her from the room. "There's a thunderstorm coming and I don't want you out in it," he warned.

"OK, darling." She smiled and left. Zander felt relieved at her departure. He didn't want to be with Tanya tonight. Tonight he wanted Mara, but she didn't want him. It bothered him greatly. He had never wanted a woman who didn't return his affections. This was new to him. What the hell was she doing to him? He didn't like it one bit.

Mara took a hot shower and crawled into bed, trying not to think of the fact that Tanya was in the house with Zander. They were probably locked up in his room doing it. She was jealous and she couldn't help it. How could he be with someone he didn't love? Was it really that easy for him to do that? She knew she couldn't. She closed her eyes and forced herself not to think about it.

Picking up her sketchpad, she started on a new chair. Sketching always took her mind off her troubles. The rain started to beat heavily against the window. A few minutes later it turned into a raging thunderstorm. She couldn't concentrate anymore. The thunder clapped and Mara cringed. She hated thunderstorms. The thunder got louder and she felt like jumping out of her skin.

The phone rang and she answered it quickly. It was Shari.

"How you holding up?" Shari asked.

"Good."

"I know how you hate thunderstorms."

"I'm handling it."

"You sure? I know you and how jumpy you get when it's thundering."

"OK, OK. How's Patrick?" she said, changing the subject.

"We'll talk when I get home." Shari sounded excited. That was a good sign. The thunder clapped and Mara moaned, wishing it would stop.

"Hang in there and if it gets bad, go find Zander— I'm sure he'd like the company."

"Tanya's already got that end covered."

"She's there?"

"Yep."

"Well, try and get some sleep, then."

"Yeah, right." Mara flinched as another thunder crackled.

"See you tomorrow."

"I'm gonna kick your behind when I see you for laughing at me!"

"Yeah, right," Shari teased.

Zander stood under the spray of the cold water. No matter how hard he tried not to think of Mara, she was all he could think of. Her beauty and intellect had captivated him in a way that he didn't expect with someone who so was not his type. Her sense of humor and sassiness had him extremely interested in getting to know her better, both physically and mentally. He smiled at the thought of her, looking up at him with those big eyes and her full, pouting lips that begged to be kissed. Zander adjusted the water and shivered under the cold spray, hoping it would cool his desires, but it was no help. He was still aroused when he got out of the shower. Knowing that she was just across the hall didn't help, either. Damn her. She had him rethinking his relationship with Tanya. He didn't ever want to fall for another woman; that was what made Tanya so perfect. She understood him and his needs. She was willing and wouldn't be a problem to him. But all he could think of was Mara and her damn questioning eyes.

The thought of her leaving after Shari's wedding bothered him. He had just met her and needed more time with her. In the few weeks she had been here, she had stepped into his every thought. How the hell did she do that, especially to a man like him?

Thunder crashed loudly and he wondered if she was asleep. He ignored the urge to go check on her as he rubbed lotion into his skin. A soft tap at his door made him look up and there she was—the sexual tormentor of his thoughts. She looked like a frightened little girl as she stepped into his room. She wore shorts and a tank that was molded to her small breasts. The thunder crashed loudly and she almost ran over to him. She was afraid of the thunder. He found it amusing.

"You alone?" she asked, quickly scanning the room.

"Yes." He grinned at the thought of her afraid of something as simple as thunder. "Couldn't sleep?"

She narrowed her eyes at him. He found her so appealing. "Don't you dare laugh at me!" she said and pointed a finger at him. He resisted the urge to go to her and take her into his arms, hug and kiss her senseless. He wanted to feel her against him, giving in to his desires. His body started to respond to his thoughts.

Mara knew she shouldn't have come to Zander's room, but she couldn't stand being alone during a thunderstorm. Plus, seeing him was always a pleasure. He was half-naked, with water dripping from his hair onto his broad chest. He wore silk boxers that hung low on his waist. She could see the line of hair on his belly disappearing into his boxers and the bulge. A pleasant shiver rang down her spine. She quickly looked elsewhere, knowing she really shouldn't have come to his room.

"Scared?" he teased.

"Smile all you want—you weren't the one who

was almost hit by lightning." She looked into his smiling eyes.

"You were almost hit by lightning?"

"On the playground in high school."

"Sorry to hear that."

"Can I stay with you until it stops?" She moaned as another clap of thunder rolled, followed by the crackling of lightning. She cringed and wrapped her arms around her body.

"You can stay, if you do my hair," he smirked.

"Resorting to blackmail, are we?"

"Good—we have a deal," he confirmed with a knowing smile. She couldn't help but laugh.

Mara sat in the armchair while Zander sat on a pillow between her legs on the floor. His skin was warm against her bare flesh. She did her best to concentrate on his hair as she towel-dried it and started to comb out the tangles. Having him so close was intoxicating, and her vivid imagination wasn't helping, either.

"How are Shari and Patrick really doing?" Zander asked suddenly.

For a moment she didn't know how to respond. "Shouldn't you be asking Shari that?"

"We don't exactly talk much, and when we do, she seems to think I'm interfering in her life."

"Are you?"

"She is my sister. I'm just concerned."

She wondered how sincere his concerns were. "If you are concerned, why don't you express that to Shari?"

"It's not that easy with her."

"You should try taking the time to talk to her. It's not that hard."

"I know, but after our parents died we kind of drifted apart."

"From what I heard, it's more like you pushed her away."

"I know, and I'm not proud of it."

Mara was surprised by his admission. "You can fix it. You two are lucky to have each other. Do you know how many times I wished I had a brother or sister to talk to?"

"Shari knows she can talk to me."

"No, she doesn't, because if she did, trust me, she would come to you."

Zander became quiet. Mara said nothing, hoping her words would sink in and he'd do something to better his relationship with his sister.

"You're right. Shari and I don't exactly communicate very well."

"So what are you going to do about it?" She ran her fingers through his now-dry hair. She loved the feel of his hair between her fingers.

"I guess I have to do something about that."

"She could use your support in more ways than money. Remember, she's all you got. You've shut her out long enough, don't you think?"

"You're right."

"Well, I'm done here," she announced.

Zander got up. She stood up, watching him run his fingers through his hair.

"Thank you." He smiled at her. She loved the way he smiled at her.

The storm was still raging outside, and she wasn't ready to leave him just yet.

"Tell you what. You've got that side of the bed,"

he told her, pointing to the left side of his king-size bed. "You don't snore, do you?"

"No." She glared at him.

"Good. I wouldn't want to have to send you to your room."

"Very funny."

"You don't kick in your sleep, do you?"

"No!"

"Good, because I wouldn't want to have to re-strain you."

Mara settled in on her side of the bed and pulled the covers up under her chin.

"Thanks and good night."

He turned out the lights and got into bed. She did feeel a lot better in his company.

"Good night, Mara," she heard him say as she closed her eyes.

Sometime during the night, Zander woke to the feel of Mara's soft body pressed into his side. One of her arms was across his chest and her nose was pressed into his arm. One of her legs was against his. He looked over at her, afraid to move. She was snoring softly, her breath warm against his flesh, which caused his skin to tingle and his blood to warm. He moved closer to her, and she shifted into him. He cradled her against him. He closed his eyes and went back to sleep.

The sound of the shower woke Mara the next morning. She was in the middle of the bed, almost on Zander's side. She hoped she hadn't disturbed him during the night. She rolled over to his side, inhaling his scent before she got up. He had been such a great comfort to her last night.

She headed into his bathroom. He was in the shower—Mara could see him clearly. A cap protected his hair. Her eyes dropped, but a towel placed just right blocked her view of his lower body. Too bad. She angled her head, hoping to get a better view.

"Morning," he said, and Mara jumped, looking into his face. He had caught her staring. She flushed.

"Morning."

"You know, you do snore."

"I wasn't too loud, was I?" she asked, a bit embarrassed.

He smiled. "No, it was kind of cute, actually."

"Snoring isn't cute," she exclaimed. "As long as I didn't keep you awake."

"No, you didn't."

"Want breakfast?"

"You don't have to."

"I would love to."

"OK. Thanks, but I only have about thirty minutes before I have to leave."

"You have enough time."

Mara made him eggs with chunky salsa mixed in, toast, and coffee. She was pouring the coffee when he walked into the kitchen dressed in his signature dark blue suit. Damn, he looked good.

"Sit," she said and gestured toward the table. He placed his jacket on the back of the chair and sat down. He smiled warmly at her, as she sat across from him with a cup of coffee.

"Thanks for putting up with me last night."

"My pleasure," he smiled. "So what are you doing today?" He began to eat his eggs.

She mimicked a British accent. "Shari's taking me shopping for Kate's tea party."

He laughed. "A woman who doesn't like shopping?"

"It's not that I don't like shopping. I just don't have the money to, and Shari has bought me some very expensive cloths already."

"You don't have to feel guilty about that."

"I don't want to take advantage of our friendship."

"You don't strike me as the type who would take advantage of anyone. Especially a friend." He was right, but she still felt a bit guilty.

He looked at his watch. "I have to go." He got up, putting on his jacket.

"I'll see you later," he said.

"Have a good day." She smiled at him. He stopped and looked at her with wonder. Then he moved over to her and leaned toward her, looking deeply into her eyes. Mara was mesmerized as she stared back up at him.

"Thanks," he whispered and kissed her so gently it took her breath away. He smiled and hurried off. Mara sighed and touched her lips, smiling. Stop it! *Remember he's trying to seduce you,* she reminded herself. She did not need to fall into his trap, no matter how nice he was to her. Or how well he kissed.

* * *

Shari called to let Mara know that their shopping spree would have to wait until the next day. She was spending some quality time with Patrick. Mara grabbed her sketchpad, deciding to work on some drawings. The phone rang on her way out to the pool. Realizing that she was the only one in the house, she answered it.

"Hello?"

"Mara?"

"Stone?" She recognized his voice.

"What are you doing for the rest of the day?"

"Nothing—Shari just cancelled on me."

"Great. I'm coming to pick you up."

"Sounds good to me." She was glad to have something to do for the day.

"I'll be there in half an hour," Stone told her.

"Should I wear anything special?"

"No, I just want to sketch you."

"Sketch me?" She had forgotten his request to do so. She thought about it and concluded there was no harm in it.

"Please let me," he pleaded gently.

"OK."

"Thank you."

Stone picked her up in his silver BMW convertible. He was dressed in pale linen, a departure from the dark colors he'd worn the last two times she saw him. He wore designer shades.

"Nice car," she said as they roared down a two-lane road. It was a clear, bright day. Mara slipped on her shades.

"Thanks." He smiled at her.

* * *

At Stone's studio, Mara wandered around, look-ing at his unfinished pieces as he gathered supplies to sketch her. He returned with a large pad that he mounted on an easel, then pulled a long chaise to the middle of the room. He then disappeared and came back with white sheets. Mara watched him as he prepared the chaise.

"OK, undress," he said.

"What?" She was shocked by his request. She didn't know he wanted to sketch her naked.

"I want to do you in the nude."

"Wow! Hold up. I didn't agree to sitting for you nude."

"It's the only way I want you. Your body is incred-ible curvaceous, and that's what I want to capture."

"I don't think so." Mara folded her arms across her chest.

"It will be very tasteful."

Mara shook her head, backing away.

"Hold on," he said and hurried over to a wall where he pulled out a charcoal sketch and showed her. "This is how I want you."

Mara stared at the nude woman in the picture. She was beautiful. She lay on her stomach on a white sheet, her eyes closed as if sleeping. It was tasteful, beautiful, and extremely exotic, all at the same time. "What do you think?"

"It's beautiful."

Stone put the sketch away. "I'll turn my back so you can undress." He turned his back to her. "Lie on the chaise with your head that way." He pointed to the right.

"Stone, I don't know."

"Please, Mara. I have to sketch you. You can have it when I'm done."

Mara looked at the sketch he had shown her. She removed her clothes, then lay down as he had instructed.

"Ready," she told him, and he turned to look at her and smiled.

"I want to adjust you a bit, is that OK?" he asked. She nodded. He moved over to her, adjusting the sheet around her. "You have great lines," he told her as he adjusted her hips. Mara gazed at him. She felt surprisingly comfortable with him. "Wonderful," he said, moving to put on some classical music before taking his spot behind his easel.

Two hours later, Stone suggested that they take a break. He handed her a robe and turned his back again. She slipped it on and secured it about her waist. He invited her into the kitchen area where he pulled out two Caesar salads and sparkling water from the refrigerator.

"I would have ordered something else, but with you lying down, you don't need anything heavy on your stomach."

"This will do," she said, enjoying her salad.

An hour later they were back to work. A couple of times Mara fell asleep. Stone assured her it was OK and kept on drawing. Occasionally she got up and stretched.

"Wake up, beautiful." Stone's breath caressed her ear. Mara opened her eyes and smiled up at him.

"Done?" she asked, turning over, holding the sheet over her breasts.

"Want to see?" he asked, getting up and holding a hand out to her. She noticed that his hands were clean of the charcoal. She wondered how long she was asleep. She took his hand while holding the sheet in front of her. He led her around to the sketch.

"Oh, my," Mara exclaimed at what she saw. It was a stunning nude replica of her—she never knew her body could look like that. The curves, the angles, it was amazing. Did she really look like that? Stone had captured every detail of her face and body. Her face was stunning, with a sultry gaze. "It's amazing," she said. She couldn't believe that he had completed the sketch in such a short time.

"What time is it?" she asked, noticing that the skyline outside his studio was dark.

"Almost eleven."

"What?" she gasped.

"Don't worry—I called the house to let them know you were with me."

Mara breathed a sigh of relief and turned back to the drawing. She still couldn't believe that she could look so good.

"You are a very beautiful woman," Stone told her stepping behind her and caressing her arms.

"You made me beautiful," she said and leaned against him. The likeness was overwhelming.

"I only drew what I saw." He kissed her neck and a shiver ran down her spine. Mara closed her eyes, enjoying the play of his lips against her skin. Stone turned her to face him. Reaching for the sheet, he pulled it from her hand, looking down at her body.

"Beautiful," he whispered and lowered his head toward her. Mara closed her eyes as his lips touched hers. His kiss was hot and hungry. Mara wrapped her arms about his neck, lost in his kiss. He pulled his mouth from hers and looked deeply into her eyes.

"I have to taste you," he said. Mara didn't know how to respond. "I know it's too soon for us, but I must taste you."

Mara was weak with a hunger that had been left unfed for a long time. Stone picked her up and took her back to the chaise. He gently placed her on her back, and moved away, looking down at her. He sat down beside her and leaned into her and kissed her with such hunger that Mara could do nothing but respond to him. She gripped his braids. Stone moved down her body. His hot, wet mouth played over her breasts, suckling her nipples into hardness. A delicious heat filled Mara and she felt a wetness flowing from her. Stone moved down her chest to her stomach, placing sweet, wet kisses over her hot flesh. Mara moaned under his delicious exploration. Her body cried out for release in the worst way. Stone gently eased her legs apart, finding her wetness. Gently his fingers explored her as he caressed her stomach with his tongue. She moaned, digging her hands into his hair. Stone moved between her legs, looking at her. Mara looked at him; she felt exposed and stimulated under his gaze. She watched as he lowered his head between her legs. She quivered and lay back, biting her lips. She felt his hair brush her inner thighs, causing her skin to tingle. His mouth touched her and Mara felt her body convulse. Skillfully, Stone's lips explored her. He gripped her thighs, caressing her flesh, then licked and suckled her into a multiple orgasm.

Later, as Mara lay breathless, Stone sat beside her, his hands gliding over her body.

"What did you do to me?" she asked, licking her dry lips.

"Have you ever had oral sex?" he asked.

"Not that good."

"Would you like more?" He caressed her bottom lip. Zander's face suddenly flashed before her. Oh, God, what had she let him do?

"I think you should take me back to the house." She sat up. Stone got up and reached for her clothes, handing them to her.

"You are not ready—I understand." He was so calm, it soothed her somehow.

"I'm sorry." She started to put on her clothes. She felt nothing but guilt.

"Don't be. You are young and haven't experienced much sexually. I could tell from your body's response."

Mara stopped and looked at him. He was right, but she wasn't about to tell him that. Mara had never had a man who satisfied her as Stone had—just with his mouth. Her mind raced at the possibility of what else he could do to her, what he could teach her. She recalled Shari telling her how seductive Stone could be. It could be so easy to let him show her, but she couldn't. It wouldn't be right. Mara slipped her feet into her mules. She felt a bit guilty about allowing him to do what he'd done to her.

"Do not feel guilty about what happened. It was a pleasure to taste you." Stone smiled.

Mara couldn't help but laugh. "You are bad for me."

"If only you'd let me be that bad." He winked at her. Mara laughed as she slipped on her shoes.

Chapter 11

Zander was late. He had told Tanya that he'd be at her condo by nine, but when he got there it was almost 10:30. He hoped she wouldn't be too upset. She opened the door on his second ring.

"Sorry I'm late." He stepped into the living room of her luxurious condo, decorated in a modern, chic style. She closed the door behind him. "I got caught up with a deal I have to finalize by next week." She moved up to him. She looked beautiful, as always, dressed in a red silk kimono. He knew she wasn't wearing anything under it.

"As long as you're here . . ." She wrapped her arms around his neck, kissing him. He eased her away from him as she tried to force her tongue into his mouth. He had reviewed their relationship on the way over and it had to end. There was nothing tangible in their arrangement, except her giving him the children he wanted to carry on his legacy.

"What's wrong?" she asked, puzzled.

"We need to talk," he started.

"We can talk later—it's been months since we've made love. I miss you—I need you, Zander." She eased the robe open, revealing her body. Her skin was tanned and smooth, her breasts large with pink nipples. He knew her body well. It would be so easy. He hadn't been with another woman since his last time with her, and that was months ago. The fact was, he didn't want her. He wanted Mara.

"I have to put an end to this," he continued.

"What?" She stepped back and glared at him. "Did you find someone else? Is that why you've been brushing me off since I got back from Paris?"

"There's no one else."

"Yes, there is, or you wouldn't be doing this," she snapped. She had a right to be angry; he was, after all, ending their agreement.

"Did you see Sean while you were in Paris?" he asked her, and she went pale. He knew she had. Sean was the reason Tanya had run off to Paris. Sean Michal was a French artist they had both met at a show in Manhattan. Zander had witnessed first-hand the interest Tanya had taken in his work. He also knew it wasn't just his work she was interested in. Sean had surrounded himself with a kind of mystique, and she had fallen for it. Then again, he couldn't blame her. There was nothing exciting about their relationship. Everything was routine, even the sex. The minute he had suspected there was something between them, he had stopped sleeping with her. And that was over four months ago. She had been in Paris for the past two months. He knew she had been with Sean. Apparently it was over, because here she was, back in Spring Lake, wanting him more than she did before. He knew better.

"Answer the question, Tanya."

"No, I did not see Sean in Paris." Her voice cracked; he knew she was lying.

"Did you sleep with him while you were there?"

"No!" she cried, devastated. "I told you—I didn't see Sean."

He calmly asked, "Why don't I believe you?"

"Zander, please. Sean was just a crush, nothing more." She pleaded for his understanding. He just couldn't believe her because he knew her too well. If Sean hadn't turned her down, she would not have returned to the States.

"He excited you enough for you to run off to Paris."

"I swear to God, Zander. Nothing happened between me and Sean, nothing." Tears surfaced—another one of her tricks, crying on cue.

"You need to stop."

"Zander, believe me. Nothing happened with Sean. He just wasn't the man I thought he was."

Zander looked at her. He knew he wasn't in love with her, but he did care about her. He had known her for so long.

"I don't love you, Tanya." He expected her to scream at him, but she didn't. She simply stared at him.

"Love was never an issue before. Why is it now?" she asked calmly. "The plan was for us to get married, and I'd provide you with children. Why are you doing this? Yes, I always knew you didn't love me, but you made a promise to me."

"Our arrangement is off."

"It's that little bitch Mara, isn't it? I've seen the way you look at her." Her eyes darkened with hate.

"She's not a bitch, and she has nothing to do with this."

"Doesn't she?" Her eyes blazed with anger.

"No, she doesn't."

"Ever since she got here, I never see you! You have cancelled every one of our dinners, giving me some bull about working at home. And what about the other night when you were out with her?"

"Shari was there also, in case you forgot."

"I know you."

"And I know that you slept with Sean."

Tanya stared at him, unable to speak.

"Well, I hope you enjoy your little ghetto bitch while it lasts."

"There's nothing ghetto about Mara, so watch your mouth!"

Tanya shook her head. "So I was right. She's the cause of your sudden change of plans."

"Good-bye, Tanya," he said and started for the door.

"You will regret this," she screamed.

He felt good about his decision and that was all that mattered. "I don't think so," he said and walked out of her condo.

Chapter 12

Mara stood staring at her sketch while she waited for Shari. She was dressed in a periwinkle pantsuit with navy blue hat, purse, and pumps. They were going to Kate's tea party.

"Oh, my, God!" Shari said, joining her.

"It is beautiful, isn't it?" She smiled.

"Are you joking? The way Stone captured you! It's amazing."

"What do you think my mother would say if she saw it?"

"That you are beautiful."

The tea party was on the Rhones' lawn. Women in fancy hats and outfits sipped tea, wine, and champagne while they munched on finger sandwiches, discussing society events and, of course, Shari's upcoming wedding.

Kate proudly showed off her soon-to-be daughter-in-law. Mara found it delightful, making small talk as she tried to figure out who was old money and who was new. The women tried to impress each other with what their husbands had acquired. After a while, Mara got bored with the pleasant conversations. Plus, her feet were starting to hurt. She ventured into a secluded part of the garden, sat on a bench, slipped off her shoes, and rubbed her feet. A few minutes later, Shari found her.

"Oh Lord, Mara, don't let Kate see you doing that," Shari exclaimed.

"Girl, please, these damn pumps are about to blind me." Shari giggled and sat beside her. "So what happened with Patrick?"

"I couldn't tell him" she responded, torn.

"But did you ask him?"

"No, we didn't exactly get around to talking too much."

"Like I said, leave it alone."

Mara saw Kate coming toward them and quickly slipped on her shoes. Kate wore a peach pantsuit with a cream-colored hat. She was always so elegant and classy.

"Mara, you don't mind me borrowing Shari for a few minutes, do you?"

"Of course not," Mara told her with a smile.

"Rotate your ankles in tiny circular motions," Kate told her with a wink and a smile. Mara was grateful she hadn't offended her. As Kate led Shari off, Mara slipped off the pumps and did as she was told, relaxing and closing her eyes.

"What are you doing here?" a familiar voice asked. She opened her eyes to find Tanya standing about ten feet away. She was dressed in a red-and-cream outfit with matching hat and shoes. Tanya looked at her with contempt, and Mara returned the look while she slipped her shoes back on and stood up to face her.

"What's it to you?"

"One would think that you would know your place."

Mara rolled her eyes as Tanya looked her over with contempt. Did this woman have to be everywhere she went? Mara knew she didn't belong in their circle, but she wasn't about to let this woman disrespect her.

"*Bitch* is your middle name, right?" Mara asked with a serious face.

Tanya's eyes narrowed. "If you think I'm going to let you take Zander from me, you are sadly mistaken," Tanya screamed.

"Are you for real?"

"You can throw yourself at him all you want, but know this. He would never want the likes of you."

How did she know that Zander wanted her? He must have said something to her. But why would he? It made no sense. Tanya was Zander's fiancée; why would he jeopardize his relationship—or "arrangement" as he put it?

"You are nothing but a little slut."

Mara snapped at attention, glaring at her. *That was it!* No one called *her* a slut. Mara stepped toward her. Suddenly Shari materialized out of nowhere, stepping between them.

"What's going on here?" Shari asked.

"She almost attacked me for no reason at all," Tanya cried, and managed to look frightened in the process.

Mara glared at Tanya, shocked at her sudden change from lioness to weakling. So that was her game. And if she thought she was going to get away with it, she had another think coming.

"I hope you don't believe this lying heifer," Mara said.

"Ghetto bitch!" Tanya suddenly yelled. Instantly Shari turned to Tanya and slapped her hard across the face. Shari's sudden action took Mara totally by surprise, but it also made her proud.

"How dare you?" Tanya asked, holding her cheek. "She's not even one of us."

"I suggest you leave before I really let Mara kick your behind," Shari told her. Mara would have loved nothing more than to give Tanya a beat-down.

"This is not the end of this!" Tanya yelled before storming off.

"Mara, I'm so sorry," Shari said. "Are you OK?"

"It's cool." Mara wasn't fazed by anything that came out of Tanya's mouth. She knew Tanya didn't like her. The feeling was mutual.

"No, it's not. I don't want anyone making you feel like you don't belong here."

"Honestly, I already know I don't, but it doesn't bother me," Mara told her with a smile and Shari smiled back, relieved. The one thing Mara had never done was lie about who she was and where she came from. She understood that coming here, she would encounter people like Tanya. Not that the encounter didn't bother her, but she wasn't about to let it get under her skin. However, she would have loved to be the one who slapped her. "You really laid one on her, didn't you?"

Shari looked guilty for a brief moment. "You know I'm not like that."

"I know, and that's what's so surprising."

"If anyone says anything to you . . ."

"Shari, I can handle myself, and you know that."

"I don't want you to be uncomfortable here," Shari insisted.

"I am not—trust me."

"What was she so upset about?"

"She thinks I'm trying to steal Zander from her."

"No," Shari said, amused.

"Oh, yeah."

"This is interesting. Why would she think that?"

"Ask your brother. And do me a favor—tell him to keep his woman in check."

"Darlings, come, come," Kate said, approaching them. "You two can't keep taking off like this." Kate ushered them back to the party. Tanya was nowhere in sight.

Chapter 13

"I heard you called," Mara said into the phone. She had returned to the mansion an hour ago to find a message from Stone.

"Mara?" Stone said.

"Yes."

"Thanks for returning my call."

"You're welcome. So what's going on?"

"I need a favor."

"Depends on if I have to take my clothes off and it involves tasting," Mara said, and he laughed.

"None of the above, I promise."

"I'm listening."

"There's a fund-raiser tomorrow night, and I need a date. Interested?"

"I'd love to." She accepted, knowing that Shari was going away for a couple of days with Patrick. She could use some distraction. She had been thinking about Zander more than she should. Then there was that Tanya issue.

"Great. I'll pick you up at six."

"OK," she told him.

"Thanks, Mara."

"See you soon," she told him and hung up the phone, only to find Shari frowning at her.

"Who was that?"

"Stone. He wants me to go to some fund-raiser event with him."

"Zander's going to be there," Shari said, alarmed.

"And?"

Shari shrugged. "Just thought you should know."

"Thanks for the heads-up."

She didn't care that Zander was going to be there. She was going with Stone and she was going to have a good time.

"Are you sure you'll be OK?" Shari asked for the fifth time as Mara helped her pack an overnight bag for her two-day escape with Patrick.

"Would you stop? This is about you and your man, not me."

"I just hate leaving you alone. It seems like I'm always leaving you alone. I'm a bad host, aren't I?" she said, looking guilty.

"No, you're not. I will be fine . . . Go be with your man. Do you think I'd be worried about you if I had a man like Patrick waiting for me?"

Shari hugged her and thanked her for understanding before she left.

Mara found Helen busier than usual in the kitchen getting ready to make dinner.

"Need any help?" she asked. Helen looked at her, flustered.

"Just making a quick dinner before I go see my grandson. He's sick."

"I'm sorry to hear that, but you do know I can make my own dinner."

"I couldn't let you do that. You're a guest."

"A guest who can cook," Mara informed her. "No one is here except me. I can manage."

"Zander should be home later."

"Just tell me what he likes. I can make it. He's not that fussy, is he?"

"No, he isn't. He likes his food simple, actually."

"Tell you what. Why don't you go be with your grandson—I can finish up here. Give me something to do, anyway. I'm not exactly used to sitting around."

"Are you sure?"

"You need to go. I will be fine. I can handle this, really."

"Thank you, honey," Helen said and hurried from the kitchen.

Helen had pulled out some chicken cutlets, vegetables, and baby potatoes. Turning the radio on and finding an R&B soul station, Mara sang along with the music as she prepared dinner.

She was checking on the potatoes when someone cleared their throat behind her. She sprung around, ready to swing at whoever it was. She sighed in relief when she saw that it was Zander. He stood watching her with a delightful look on his face.

"I must be a lucky man. First breakfast, now dinner." He moved toward her. She watched him, thinking how handsome he was. He had discarded his jacket, his tie was loose, and the first two buttons on his shirt were undone. His hair was loose about his shoulders. He was a man she could definitely look at every day with pleasure.

"Helen told me what you were doing," he said.

"It's no big deal."

"Thank you."

"The potatoes aren't quite done yet. You can go change if you like."

"I'll do just that." He left the room. Mara resumed her singing and started to set the table. Then she ran upstairs to wash her face and change from her T-shirt into a soft blue peasant-style blouse. She brushed back her hair, adding styling gel to hold it in place. Adding a touch of lip gloss, she paused to look at the image in the mirror. Her eyes were filled with excitement, and she knew Zander was the cause of it.

"Be careful, girl," she told herself. She knew Zander was attracted to her, but she also knew she should be on guard. Zander could get any woman he wanted, so why the interest in her? She wasn't tall, leggy or blond with huge breasts, like his woman. She wasn't even in his class. She really had to stay focused when it came to Zander, or he'd succeed at seducing her. Not that it was a bad thing, but he was engaged. She had to remember that.

In the kitchen she found Zander pouring red wine. He looked up at her and smiled, and offered her a glass. She took it, and took a sip. The wine was dry, yet rich in flavor. He was staring again. She watched as he looked her over slowly. It sent warmth through her. How could he do that just by looking at her?

"Is there anything that you don't do well?" he asked as he ate her baked chicken, which was accompanied by spicy baby potatoes and sautéed vegetables.

"I'm going to take that as a compliment."

"Please do. It's delicious." He smiled sexylike at her. "I'd like to ask a favor, if you don't mind."

"Haven't heard it yet."

"I need a date for tomorrow night. It's a fund-raiser."

He was asking her out on a date and she was beyond flattered. But why wasn't he taking Tanya?

"What about Tanya?"

"I'm not seeing her anymore." He looked right at her as he said it. Mara was shocked; it took her a moment to process what he had just said. Then it all came together. He had broken up with Tanya and, of course, she blamed her. No wonder the woman was so hostile toward her.

"What, why?"

"You were right—I wouldn't be happy with her. I would only be fooling myself."

He had actually listened to her—again, she was surprised.

"Did you happen to mention my name when you were breaking up with her?"

"No, I didn't," he responded. Mara didn't believe him. That had to be it, or Tanya wouldn't have gone off on her the way she did. She still couldn't believe he had ended his relationship just like that. She wondered what was the real reason behind the breakup.

"You sure about that?"

"Yes," he insisted.

"She accused me of stealing you from her."

"Did she?" He seemed amused.

"You must have given her some reason for her to think that."

"Tanya was always the paranoid type. So what's your answer?"

"About what?" Mara asked, confused.

"Tomorrow night?"

"I'd love to, but I can't," she said. "I, I already told Stone I'd be his date."

"I see," he said, disappointed. His face went completely cold. "Well, thanks again for the dinner." He got up and abruptly walked away.

Mara was so shocked by his behavior. It took her a while to digest what had just happened. Damn, he could be so rude. What the hell was his problem? She took a deep breath and calmed down. He wasn't worth all that energy, anyway. She would not give him a second thought, she just wouldn't. The less she thought of Zander or his strange behavior, the better. She wanted to scream at him, but of course, he was gone.

Mara cleared the table, loaded the dishwasher, and headed upstairs. He was obviously mad at her for going to the fund-raiser with Stone. Was Zander jealous? He wasn't the type; he was far too cold for that. But he had no right to be giving her attitude over that, and that had rattled her.

Mara watched TV for a few hours, then decided to go for a swim. She changed into her tankini and headed downstairs. She was passing Zander's office when the door opened and he came out.

"Going for a dip?" he asked as his eyes moved over her body at a luxurious pace. She reminded herself of his previous behavior and the fact that she was mad at him.

"Yeah," she responded dryly and headed out to the pool. The water was cool and refreshing as Mara floated on her back, looking up into the early night sky. She heard a splash and looked to see Zander swimming her way. She got out of his way and watched him swim the length of the pool before surfacing a few feet from her. He pushed his hair back. God, he was sexy. She watched him closely as he floated a few feet away from her before standing up. She stared at him.

"You shouldn't swim alone," he said, pressing water from his hair.

"I'm fine at the shallow end."

He walked over to her. Mara didn't move; she couldn't, as she was in a corner. He reached out and pulled her against him. His body was rock hard against hers. Mara looked up at him. The light bounced off his bronze skin and his eyes shimmered as they held her captive. He pulled her closer and she felt his hardened sex against her stomach. She swallowed and closed her eyes, holding back a moan. She kept her eyes closed as his lips took hers. He kissed her deeply and slowly until her senses spun out of control. Mara wrapped her arms about his neck, as he lifted her against him. Her sexual hunger raced through her like wildfire. He cupped her left breast, caressing her gently. Zander quickly broke the kiss and pulled her top down, exposing her breasts. Mara gasped as he lowered his head to her breasts. His entire mouth engulfed her breasts, suckling hungrily. His other hand cupped her rear and pressed her into his hardened sex. Mara's mind reeled with the pleasure he lavished on her body. She gripped his hair, pressing his face into her breasts. She moaned his name.

"Let's get out of here," he told her. They left the pool, stopping briefly to wash, before toweling off. Zander lifted Mara and carried her inside. Mara buried her face into his neck, kissing his damp skin as she ran her fingers through his hair. Zander took her upstairs and into his room, then placed her on his bed. His mouth covered hers and Mara opened up, welcoming his hot tongue. His hands explored her body, caressing her breasts. Her nipples hardened under his searching touch. His hand covered her sex, and he caressed her through the material that covered her. Then his fingers found their way beneath her suit and sank into her wet sex. She heard him moan. Mara pressed up into his hand as a finger slipped into her, massaging gently. His mouth left hers to find her breasts. He pulled back and removed her suit, then got up and started to remove his trunks. Mara gasped, afraid of what she was about to do with him. As if sensing her fear, Zander stopped.

"You're not ready for this," he said. Mara looked at him, unsure. As much as she wanted Zander, she wasn't sure if it was right. Zander stepped away, allowing Mara to get up. She grabbed her suit and ran out of his room, her heart beating a mile a minute. Her body craved him in the worst way. But it was too dangerous to get involved with him. She took a long shower, trying to forget his touch, his kiss, the feel of his body, but she couldn't. She wanted him so much, it hurt. She just couldn't let it happen. What the hell was he doing to her?

Chapter 14

It was almost eleven when she made it downstairs the next day. She had spent half the night thinking of Zander and what had almost happened between them. She felt like packing and going back to D.C., but she couldn't. She had come here for Shari. She couldn't disappoint her best friend. It was killing her, wanting him the way she did. She knew he wasn't going to stop until he had her in his bed. And as much as she wanted him, she had to deny him. She also knew that if he hadn't stopped last night, they would have made love. She really had to find a way to stay away from Zander. She thought of Stone. He was definitely not the answer, especially after what she allowed him to do to her. However, he was still her best distraction.

After a late breakfast, she decided to sketch by the pool. A few hours later, she ventured down to the gym in the basement, which also housed a wine cellar and a huge pantry.

The gym had an array of different exercise machines. Mara got on one of the high-tech treadmills, and after pressing a few buttons, she got the thing going. She did the treadmill for thirty minutes, then she got on a mat and did some crunches. She showered and settled for some fruit salad. She was about to go out to the pool when Helen walked in.

"Everything's OK?" Helen looked at her, concerned.

"Yes. How's your grandson?"

"His fever broke, thank God." She sighed in relief.

"Sit—let me get you some coffee," Mara offered.

"It's OK, I can get it."

"Helen, sit," Mara said sternly, and Helen collapsed into a chair at the table. Mara poured her a steaming cup of coffee—black with sugar, just how Helen liked it.

"Thank you. You are such a darling," Helen told her as she handed her the cup.

"You're welcome."

"Zander wasn't too much for you last night, was he?"

"No."

"Thanks again for taking care of him. He can be a handful sometimes. Especially when he gets moody."

"What's his sign?"

"Gemini."

"That explains the attitude changes."

"So what would you like for dinner tonight?"

"I'm going to a fund-raiser with Stone. Zander's going to be there also, so you can get some rest."

"Oh, yes! I forgot about the fund-raiser dinner," Helen said, sipping her coffee. "So you're going with Stone?" Helen eyed her over the mug.

"Something wrong with Stone?" Mara was curious as to why Shari, Zander, and now Helen, all seemed to have something against her going out with Stone.

"No, he's a nice man."

"That's what everyone says, but I get the feeling no one wants me around him. Why?"

"I thought you liked Zander."

"Zander?" Mara laughed nervously.

"Yes, Zander." Helen eyed her curiously.

"I like Zander. But not the way you think." She shifted, uncomfortable with the subject.

"Could have fooled me," Helen murmured.

She did like Zander, but she wasn't about to admit that to anyone.

"Zander is not my type. Plus, I'd be only fooling myself with a man like him."

"And why would you think that?"

"Come on, Helen. I'm not even in Zander's league."

"Is that what you think?"

"It's what I know. We don't exactly match."

"I think you do," Helen said and walked off. Mara thought about what Helen had just said, but she knew Helen was wrong. They were too different and it would never work.

Mara chose a charcoal satin dress that was one-shouldered. The dress enhanced her breasts and waist to perfection before falling into a full skirt to her ankles. She wore black sling-back leather pumps with a matching purse. She borrowed Shari's platinum drop earrings and a necklace to match. She had wrapped her hair from the night before, so all she had to do was brush it into place. Done, she stood back and looked at her reflection in the mirror. She looked good. She checked to make sure she looked good from every angle, especially from behind. Everything was nice and smooth back there.

Mara heard the doorbell and picked up her purse and left her room. As she passed Zander's room, he stepped out into the hallway. They both stopped and stared at each other. He was handsomely dressed in a charcoal gray suit with a white shirt and black tie. His face was clean-shaven, his hair pulled back in a neat ponytail. Damn, he looked good. *Stay focused. He's off limits.*

"You look incredible." He smiled, looking her over.

"Thank you—you don't look so bad yourself," she told him, and his smile widened at her compliment. Hearing Stone's voice, Mara headed downstairs. Stone stood in the foyer, dressed in a tux. He looked up, saw her, and smiled. Mara smiled at him as she came to a stop before him. Stone kissed her cheek, looking at her, amazed.

"God, you look so beautiful."

"Thank you." She kept the smile on her face and forced herself not to look back at Zander. She felt him behind her. Stone looked over at Zander.

"Zander," Stone said, acknowledging Zander.

"Stone." Zander moved up beside Mara. She gazed at Zander. Suddenly she wanted to be with him, not Stone. She instantly looked back at Stone. She was his date tonight and she would concentrate on him.

The two men shook hands.

"Ready?" Stone asked.

"Yes," she said. He offered her an arm and she took it.

"Thanks for being my date on such short notice." Stone took her hand, caressing it as they sat in the back of a private car.

"I'm on vacation. There isn't much I have to do, anyway."

"Is that the only reason you accepted my invite?"

"No. If I didn't like you, trust me, I wouldn't have accepted."

"So you do like me?" His eyes sparkled with glee.

"Don't twist it," she said with a smile. He laughed.

"That's why I like you. You don't miss a thing."

"And don't forget it," she warned with a smile.

The fund-raiser was at a hall on Wreck Pond. The gardens on the grounds were in full bloom; the sun was setting and the view was spectacular.

"This place would be great for a wedding," Mara commented, thinking of Shari.

"Isn't it?" Stone looked at her.

"Oh, don't even start." She nudged him and he laughed, then led her inside. They made their way through a grand foyer and into a ballroom. Tables were set up with glowing centerpieces of colorful flowers and candles.

Kate approached them. She was stunning in a powder blue satin dress and diamonds.

"Darling, you look wonderful," Kate said and kissed Mara's cheek. Mara blushed at her compliment. Kate never failed to make her feel welcome, which Mara appreciated.

A main table was set up at the front of the room where six men sat. She noticed an empty seat at the end of the table.

Stone took her to a table where an older African-American couple sat. Stone introduced them to her as Raven and Luc Harris. The Harrises were close friends of the Tuskcan family and had heard about her. She was flattered by their warm, friendly welcome.

Mara noticed Zander the minute he entered the room. His height and good looks made him stand out like a sore thumb. She watched him as he smiled and greeted people. He took the last seat at the head table. He briefly greeted the man next to him, and then he looked right at her. He gave her a knowing smile and her heart raced. She looked away.

Stone and Luc were engaged in some conversation that Mara had zoned out on. She forced herself not to look at Zander again.

"He's staring again," Raven whispered, and Mara looked at Raven, a bit alarmed. Then she returned her attention to Zander. He was staring at her, and this time when their eyes met, he looked away. Mara turned to Raven. "So you're the one," Raven whispered.

"Sorry?" Mara asked, confused, looking into Raven's jet-black eyes. Raven was looking at her as if she knew her thoughts; it sent chills down her spine.

The ceremony started, and Mara focused on the key speaker, a short, fat Italian man. After a number of speeches, Zander took the microphone. Mara felt her pulse race as his baritone voice eased its way over the crowd. Stone shifted his chair closer to her, and Mara gazed at him with a soft smile. Zander was thanking everyone for their donations and the time they had given to the cause of children with cancer. His eyes came to rest on her as he spoke, but only for a brief moment. He was a magnificent speaker, and she enjoyed listening to him. When he was done, everyone applauded. The MC then announced it was time for dinner as soft music floated about the room.

Dinner was served, but Mara barely ate. She couldn't stop thinking of what Raven had said about her being the one. She wanted to ask her what she meant, but she was afraid to.

After dinner, Stone took her around the room, introducing her to various people. Mara was laughing at a joke Stone had told a Chinese couple when she saw Tanya.

Tanya wore a red dress that flattered her in every way. Mara watched her closely as she made her way over to them. She wondered what stunt she was going to pull next.

"Stone, darling," she cooed and kissed Stone right on the mouth before he could react. Mara knew exactly what she was doing. A part of her wanted to laugh at Tanya's childish game. The other part wanted to kick her behind. Stone wasn't her man, so she let it go.

"Tanya." Stone wiped at his mouth with a napkin

he was using to hold his drink. Tanya looked her up and down coldly. Mara moved closer to Stone, caressing his arm and glaring at her.

Tanya took a glass of red wine from a passing waiter and took a sip. Mara kept her eyes on her. She was up to something. Mara could see it in her eyes.

"Can we talk?" Tanya asked, taking hold of Stone's arm. Stone pulled his arm from her grasp none too gently, frowning at her. A few people took an interest in what was going on.

"Can't you see I'm with Mara?" Stone was irate, which brought them more attention. Tanya looked embarrassed as she glanced around, laughing nervously.

"Stone, darling, this will only take a minute. I'm sure she won't mind," Tanya said, and moved up to him, rubbing her breasts against his arm. The nerve. Stone sighed, frustrated.

"Why don't *you* excuse us?" Stone said to Tanya. He took Mara's arm and started to lead her off.

"Stone, wait!" Tanya cried out, and Stone turned to look at her. Mara had to turn with him. And that was when it happened. Tanya pretended to trip, and her red wine went down the front of Mara's dress. Mara gasped when the cold liquid hit her. Shocked, she looked at her dress in disbelief. She looked up to see a smirk forming on Tanya's face. She could not believe what Tanya had just done to her.

"Oh, sorry. It was an accident." Tanya covered her mouth, hiding her smile. Mara took one step toward her, ready to swing, and stopped when she realized where she was. She looked around to find everyone looking at them. Mara saw Zander looking at her. When his expression revealed nothing, she looked away, angry.

"Are you OK?" Stone asked.

Suddenly Kate was beside her. "Come, dear, let me take you to the lounge." Kate put an arm about her waist and led her off.

"It was an accident," she heard Tanya saying.

"No, it wasn't," she heard Stone retaliate.

Mara was so infuriated, she couldn't speak. Kate took her to the bathroom and did her best to clean off the dress with a damp cloth, but it was ruined. Mara suddenly felt like crying.

"I should have kicked her behind." Angry tears burned Mara's eyes. She could kick herself for not seeing Tanya's little stunt coming.

"You mean her ass," Kate said. Mara looked at her, grateful for her understanding.

"I don't want to offend anyone around here."

"Who cares? They could all use some offending." Kate smiled at her, and Mara felt a little better. But she was still angry. Tanya had gotten her good, and she wanted revenge.

"Has she always been a bitch, or is it just me?"

"She's always been like that, but never so vicious. What happened between you two?"

"She thinks I'm trying to steal Zander from her."

"Did you?"

Mara hesitated before responding. "He's not in my league."

Kate smiled at her. "You know, I wasn't born into all this. I kind of fell into it."

"Really?" Mara surely couldn't tell. Kate was by far the most regal woman she had ever met. One would never know she hadn't come from money.

"Really. I was a waitress when I met Rhone. His car had a flat and he didn't have a spare, so he came into the diner where I worked while in community college. First and only white man I was ever instantly attracted to. Still am." Kate smiled and moved to wet the cloth again. "Even though I'm half white and Rhone had Black in his family, his parents still didn't accept me right away. I was too local for their son. I tried to fit in as best I could, but I was starting to lose who I really was in the process. So one day I said to hell with it. I was going to be myself no matter what or whom I offended. Rhone still gets a kick out of me giving people a piece of my mind," Kate said.

"I commend you, but I don't think I could deal with it."

"If you love him, it won't matter."

"Love him?" Mara asked, surprised at her words.

"He can be a bit cold, but his heart is good. I've seen the way he looks at you."

Mara looked at Kate, not knowing what to say. First it was Helen, then Raven, and now Kate; was there something they knew that she didn't? Yes, she liked Zander, but what they were talking about was something completely different. Something she couldn't even fathom.

"There's nothing between us." Mara tried to keep her emotions from showing, but from Kate's expression, she knew she didn't believe her.

"I don't think I can do much more with your

dress." Kate stepped back. Mara looked at the long red stain down the front of her beautiful dress.

"I can't go back out there looking like this."

"I'm afraid not, dear."

Mara felt the tears roll down her cheeks. She wanted to tear Tanya apart.

"Don't cry, dear. She's not worth your tears."

Angry, Mara brushed her tears away. Kate was right. Tanya wasn't worth her tears, but she had succeeded in ruining her night and that made her mad enough to cry. As she gazed down at her dress, she realized that there was nothing she could do but go home with her tail between her legs. Next time, she would be prepared.

The bathroom door opened and Zander walked in. Their eyes met and held. He looked at her dress. Mara brushed at the tears that wouldn't stop running down her cheeks. She didn't want him seeing her crying over something as trivial as a ruined dress.

"Zander, dear, you do know that you are in the ladies' room?" Kate said to him, but Zander didn't seem to notice or care. His eyes softened as he looked at Mara, who felt warm under his gaze. The things this man could make her feel just by looking at her!

"Can you give us a minute, Kate?" Kate looked from Mara to Zander before she left.

Zander walked up to her, looking down at her dress, then into her eyes.

"Can you take me back to the house?" she asked gently. Her lips trembled as she tried to control her tears.

"What about Stone? You did come with him."

"Do I look like I care about that right now?" she snapped as the tears refused to stop coming. What was wrong with her?

Zander pulled out his handkerchief, took her chin in his hand, and wiped her tears away. She sniffled, looking up at him. He smelled wonderful and having him this close to her was soothing. He stopped wiping her face and looked into her eyes, then he lowered his head. Mara knew she should stop him, but she couldn't. His warm lips gently touched hers and she moaned softly, leaning into him. She needed him so badly.

"You little whore!" Tanya's unmistakable voice screamed. Mara jumped back to find Tanya storming at them. Zander stepped between them, but Mara came around him and swung at her. Mara had had enough. The force of her slap sent Tanya stumbling backward as she lost her balance and fell hard on her behind.

"Next time, I'll kick your . . ." she spat. "Bitch, you aren't even worth it!" Mara stepped back, controlling her anger.

"*Do* something," Tanya screamed at Zander from the floor, holding her cheek.

"Do *what*?" he asked, his voice laced with anger. He moved up to Mara and placed an arm about her waist. Mara looked at him, grateful for his support. Zander ushered her from the room, leaving Tanya on her ass, screaming obscenities at them.

Stone and Kate were outside the bathroom when they walked out.

"Are you OK?" Stone rushed to her, looking concerned.

Mara nodded. "I'm fine," she told him. All she wanted was to leave.

"I'm taking her home," Zander said.

"I can take her," Stone insisted.

Zander frowned at him. "I don't think so."

"I'll be OK," Mara told Stone and kissed his cheek. "Thanks for everything. I hope I didn't spoil your night." Stone looked at her, disappointed. Mara felt bad about leaving him, but she couldn't return to the party looking the way she did. She just wanted to go back to the mansion and forget about tonight.

Mara sat in the passenger seat of Zander's Jaguar. She had never ridden in a Jaguar before. The car was very stylish, the ride extremely smooth. Zander said nothing as he drove to the mansion. She welcomed the silence.

"I'm sorry. I shouldn't have let her get to me like that." She rubbed her hand, which still stung from the slap she had laid on Tanya earlier.

"She deserved it, after what she did tonight."

Mara gazed at him, grateful that he was on her side. She recalled the soft touch of his lips and she shivered. He gazed at her longingly. She shivered again as a wave of desire ignited in her.

"Cold? I can turn on the heat," he offered.

"No, I'm fine." She turned her face away from him, not wanting him to see the desire in her eyes. The desire she felt for him was growing, and it was starting to scare her.

At the mansion Zander assisted her from the car. The night air was cool against her bare shoulders. She wrapped her arms around herself as he came up to her, dropping his jacket over her shoulders.

"Thanks," she whispered and started for the stairs. The warmth of his jacket was welcome as her wet dress was giving her the chills. Inside, Mara started to take off his jacket, but he took hold of the lapels and pulled her toward him. She made no attempt to stop him. His mouth swooped down on hers in a heated kiss. She had to lean into him as her knees went weak. His tongue plunged into her mouth, caressing hers. She welcomed his sensuous exploration. Mara trembled against him as a wave of desire made her toes curl. She moaned softly and sagged against his hard body. Her arms were trapped inside his jacket so she couldn't touch him as she longed to. Zander slowly pulled back, which disappointed her. Her head was spinning with her need for him. He took her face in his hands and looked deep into her eyes.

"I don't want you to do anything you're not ready for. But if you are, I want you to go to my room and wait for me."

"I . . ."

"Don't say anything." He kissed her gently, silencing her before releasing her.

He was giving her a chance to think about it, and she appreciated that. But she wanted him tonight.

He ushered her up the stairs. As Mara climbed each stair, her heart raced like crazy. She couldn't look back out of fear. She had come to a crossroads with Zander, and she had to make the right decision.

* * *

Zander stood watching Mara go up the stairs, her hips swaying seductively. Silently he prayed she would be in his room when he got there. He went to his library and poured himself a drink, which he downed in one swig. If he made love to her tonight, everything would change. He recalled the image of her as he left his room earlier. She had taken his breath away in that dress. He had wanted to rip it from her body and make love to her right there and then, but Stone had shown up. He hated the fact that Stone invited her to the fund-raiser first, but the one thing he knew was that he was not going to let Stone take her home tonight. He would have found some way to get her away from him. Tanya's jealousy had worked in his favor tonight. Zander wanted Mara so badly his entire body hurt. He poured himself another drink.

Mara sat on the edge of the bed, trying not to overanalyze her situation. She dropped back onto the bed, looking up at the ceiling, sighing heavily.

"Having second thoughts?" his deep voice asked. She sat up and smiled at him. Tonight, she would be his. That was the decision she had made. She wanted him too badly to deny her feelings anymore.

"No," she whispered, and stood up facing him. He wrapped his arms about her, almost lifting her off her feet, and devoured her lips. Mara was in heaven.

Mara almost ripped the shirt off his back, wanting to get to his flesh. She lavished kisses all over his bare chest and stomach, loving the feel of his smooth, bronze skin under her hands and mouth. She unbuckled and unzipped his pants and eased them over his hips until they fell to his feet. He moaned under her touch. He wore silk boxers, and she could see the evidence of his desire pressing out against the silk. She hooked her fingers into the waist of his boxers and eased it down. He took her breath away. He was so magnificent and inviting. She touched him everywhere she could, stroking his hard flesh with the gentlest fingers. She eased her fingers into the straight, soft hair surrounding his sex. He moaned deep in his throat. Suddenly he pulled her to her feet and against him. He reached down and pulled her dress up and over her head. She stood before him, wearing only her thong. He stepped back and slowly looked her over. She loved the way he looked at her body with such approving, hungry eyes. She liked the glow of his bronze skin under the light, beads of sweat glistening off his muscles. He was a feast for the eyes—all muscles, and all man. All hers.

He picked her up and placed her in the middle of the bed, coming down on top of her. His body was hard and warm against hers. She wanted him so badly, she could barely wait to have him inside her. She trembled with anticipation.

His hands and mouth were hungry as they explored her body, heightening her passion. She wrapped her arms and legs around him, moving seductively under him. She was letting her body tell him what she wanted. His erection was pressed against her navel. She reached for him, wrapping her fingers around him. He moaned deeply, suckling at her breasts even harder. He eased her thong off.

"Zander, please," she pleaded when he slipped a finger into her. "Do you have protection?" she whispered against his neck, as she gently caressed his skin with her lips. He moaned softly against her breasts.

In a flash he jumped up and reached into the night table drawer for a condom; then he was back over her. She took it, and he sat back, looking at her. Mara opened the silver packet, then caressed him as she rolled the protection onto him. She loved the feel of him in her hands. He was solid and strong, and she couldn't wait to feel him inside her.

"Enough," he cried in frustration and pushed her back onto the bed, coming down on top of her. Mara smiled at his impatience. She looked down at him as he started to enter her body. He pressed gently into her, inch by inch. She was a little embarrassed at how tight she was, but finally he was embedded deeply in her. She sighed in total satisfaction. He was exactly what she had wanted for a long time. She wrapped her legs around him and moved her hips upward, meeting his deep thrust.

Their passion for each other was raw and untamed as they moved against each other. Each meeting the other's thrusts. Each taking and giving in return. Mara held on to him, crying out his name as she climaxed beneath him. Moments later,

Zander found his release. He squeezed her to him, breathing hard and fast. Mara had completely melted against him. The sheer bliss she felt made her unable to move. He rolled off her and pulled her into his arms, cradling her against him. Mara smiled, wrapping her arms around him as she closed her eyes.

Chapter 15

Mara woke to the scent of fresh coffee. She moaned and stretched luxuriously. She felt utter bliss. She never thought making love could ever make her feel so good. She opened her eyes, smiling to find Zander with a steaming cup over her and a sexy grin curling his lips. He wore only his pj bottoms. His hair was tucked behind his ears. Damn, he looked so good. She sat up and the sheet fell away from her body, revealing her breasts. He looked at her. She pulled the sheet up and tucked it under her arms, covering herself. His eyes met hers and he handed her the cup.

"Thank you." She took a sip of the rich coffee. He reached for a tray and placed it across her lap. On the tray was a breakfast of mini-muffins, coffee, and juice.

"Thank you." She smiled at him.

She hungrily ate a piece of apple muffin as he sipped some juice. "So, any regrets?" he asked.

"Hell, no," she grinned. "As a matter of fact, I don't think I've ever had it that good."

He blushed. "You flatter me," he said.

"I'm not lying. I wouldn't lie about that."

He blushed some more, and she thought he was the finest man alive.

A mysterious smile played on his lips. "I love the way you get all hot and wet." His lips curled in a sexy snarl. She flushed. Now she was embarrassed, but flattered at the same time.

"You do?"

"Yes, I do," he answered in a sultry tone that made her moan. He knew exactly what he had done to her last night.

"It's all on you." She allowed the sheet to fall away. His eyes fell to her breasts. A soft moan escaped him. Her nipples hardened under his gaze. Slowly, his eyes came back to her face.

"Have you ever truly let go?"

"What do you mean?" she inquired as she felt her body starting to heat up. Last night had been amazing and she wanted more.

"I know the first time with someone new tends to be a little awkward."

"You think I was holding back?" she asked, surprised yet intrigued by his comment.

"You were holding back your screams," he said. "I'd like to hear what I'm doing to you."

"So you like a screamer?" She ran her tongue over her bottom lip. "So, would you like me to scream for you now?" She placed a foot against his hardening sex and rubbed gently. He grabbed her foot, holding it against his throbbing manhood. A moan escaped his throat as she pressed gently. His eyes darkened with desire.

"Oh, you are not playing fair." He grinned.

"Please, make me scream," she begged breathlessly. He immediately set the tray aside, put on a condom, and ripped the sheets from her body. Then he was inside her, hard and fast. It was crazy, wild, and out of control to the point where she scratched his back as he did make her scream.

An hour later, Zander and Mara finally got out of bed to shower together. Mara was soaping Zander's back, careful of where she had scratched him.

"I'm going to see Raven and Luc. I was wondering if you'd like to come with me," he asked as he slowly soaped her breasts. She moaned, enjoying his cleansing caresses.

"No office today?"

"No."

"I'd love to come," she whispered as she wrapped her fingers around his sex. She heard his gasp and smiled.

"What are you . . . " His voice trailed off as she stroked him to full hardness. He moaned softly against her neck and lifted her, pressing her into the wall. Suddenly he swore under his breath, pulled back and turned the pipe off. He lifted her and walked out of the shower with her straight into the bedroom, where he placed her onto the bed. He reached for a condom. Moments later she guided him into her with one fluid movement. He filled her and she exhaled sharply.

"Mara." He cried her name as she tightened her legs around his waist, moving with him. His lips engulfed hers and Mara lost all sense of herself.

Chapter 16

Mara admired Zander as he easily maneuvered his Jaguar on the country road toward Raven and Luc's home. The countryside they drove through was absolutely beautiful, with green, rolling lands and farm animals scattered here and there. She wore a long linen skirt with a denim vest and a baseball cap that had the Howard University logo on the front. She had left her skirt half buttoned down the front. Occasionally Zander reached over to caress her thigh. She welcomed and enjoyed his touch. He was an incredible lover and he knew exactly how to please her. She'd never had that before with any man. She had never felt so contented and happy. The things he had made her feel were mind-bending. Too bad it would end soon. But for now she'd simply enjoy her time with him.

"How long have Raven and Luc been together?" she asked, not wanting to think too much about her return to D.C.

"They've been married over forty years."

"Wow, forty years. That's amazing," she said. "How long have you known them?"

"All my life—Luc and my father were like brothers. They went to the same high school and college. Luc studied medicine and my father business. Luc's a retired surgeon, but he runs a small practice in town."

"And Raven?"

"She's a retired nurse."

"She's very interesting."

"She's also psychic."

"I thought there was something different about her." Mara recalled the way Raven had looked at her and what she'd said about her being "the one" at the fund-raiser. The memory of it sent chills down her spine.

Ten minutes later they arrived at Raven and Luc's ranch-style house, which was very modern with a uniquely curved roof. Garden paths accentuated by a mountain backdrop surrounded the house. Raven opened the front door as Zander was about to knock, greeting them with a huge smile.

"Zander, Mara." She held her arms out to Zander, who moved into them and greeted her with a loud kiss on the cheek that made her giggle. Raven looked right at Mara as if she knew all her secrets. It made Mara a bit nervous.

"Come in, come in." She ushered them inside.

"Luc, Zander and Mara are here," Raven called out, and moments later Luc emerged. His long white hair was loose and he looked like an elderly Indian chief. Zander hugged him close. Luc turned to her.

"Mara, how are you?" Luc asked.

"I'm fine," she said and smiled at him.

"Come help me in the kitchen, love. Let the men talk," Raven said and ushered her out of the room. The kitchen was spacious and decorated in oak, giving it an outdoorsy feel. Large windows looked out onto the woods in the distance.

"You have a beautiful home."

"Thank you. Zander designed it and had it built for us for our twenty-fifth anniversary."

Mara was impressed. She didn't know he had skills like that.

Raven was grilling fish steaks on a griddle on top of the stove while tossing a salad. "Tell me about you and Zander."

She recalled what Zander had told her. "Shouldn't I be asking you that?" Mara smiled at her and Raven laughed.

"Last night you were one."

Mara's heart suddenly started racing. How did she know that? Then again, Zander had told her Raven was psychic. But how could she have seen all that?

"How do you know that?"

"I felt it the moment I opened the door. You were both different. I saw something in Zander's eyes I hadn't seen before."

Mara swallowed hard, not knowing what to say.

"Don't be afraid of what you feel for him," Raven continued in a serious tone. It gave Mara the chills.

"I leave soon."

"Don't let that stop the flow, because it's a beautiful thing that you two share." Raven winked at her with a smile and Mara suddenly felt enlightened.

Zander and Luc walked into the kitchen, laughing.

"So what are we having? I'm starved," Zander announced, looking right at her. Mara blushed. They hadn't eaten anything since last night, and breakfast was, of course, ignored. Mara saw Raven's smile widen.

Lunch was grilled lemon fish with baked potatoes and salad complemented by tall glasses of iced tea. Mara noticed that Zander was relaxed and very talkative. Raven showed them new pictures of her seven grandchildren. Raven and Luc had two daughters and three sons, all professionals living in various states.

"What are you thinking?" Zander asked as they drove back to the mansion.

"How wonderful and how in love Raven and Luc are."

"Yeah. Nice, isn't it?" A moment of silence passed between them.

"Very." She sighed. "What about your parents? How long were they together?" she asked. He didn't answer, so she gazed at him. He wore a blank expression. She regretted asking him, especially because of the tragic manner in which his parents had died. "Sorry if I brought up unpleasant memories."

"No, you didn't," he said. "My parents knew each other since they were kids. They got married right out of high school. While my father was in business school at Columbia, my mother studied art at New York University. She did most of the paintings in the mansion."

"She's Dancer?" Mara asked, surprised, recalling the signature on most of the paintings on the walls.

"That's her," he said proudly. "She was a dancer at heart. She loved ballet but an injury kept her from pursuing dance."

"Wow."

"Of course, neither Shari nor I got any of her talent," he said as a bittersweet expression crossed his face.

"You miss them, don't you?"

"Every day." She heard the pain in his voice.

"They loved each other?"

"Yeah. They did everything together. They even died together." He cleared his throat. "Too bad that kind of love doesn't exist in these days." His voice was tight and cold.

"And you don't believe in love?"

"I'm sure it exists for some people but not for me. Nowadays, women don't care whose heart they break as long as they get what they want."

"That's unfair. Not all women are like that." She didn't appreciate his views on women.

"That's all I see these days. There is no real love anymore."

He didn't believe in love, and that meant he wasn't capable of loving any woman. She wondered how anyone could live without love. Even though she had seen her father walk out on her mother, Janice had told her not to judge all men by his actions. She had seen true love in many couples and she knew she'd find it one day.

"What about Shari and Patrick? They love each other."

"Since they were young, so they're different. These days it's all about what one person can get from the next."

"That's why you should be careful of who you decide to marry."

"Even in marriage there's no guarantee that person will be loyal."

"With that kind of outlook, how do you even intend to find the right woman?"

After a moment he responded, "Finding a woman is not a problem for me."

Mara looked at his handsome face, considered his wealth, and knew he was right. But she couldn't help being bothered by the fact that he could live his life without the true love of a woman. Mara could never see herself with a man whom she didn't love.

"Are we going to talk about last night?" he said. Mara looked at him, knowing she had to be guarded with him. His views on relationships had turned on her warning light.

"I'd rather not," she responded.

"Why?" His voice was tight, almost cold. What the hell did he expect from her, after telling her he didn't believe in love.

"There's no denying the chemistry between us, but I don't think we should take it too seriously."

"This is a first," he said in disbelief.

"I'm not about to get all caught up in this fantasy."

"Fantasy?"

"I come from a whole different world compared to what you live in," she told him. "Granted it's all good playing dress-up and partying, but my life is in D.C., not here. I'm not about to fool myself about you."

"I see," he commented coldly.

His jaw twitched rapidly as he focused on the road ahead. She looked away from him. Sure they had made a connection in bed, but what else was there? And she sure as hell wasn't going to start fantasizing about them being together, knowing that was downright impossible. Men like Zander didn't marry women like her; they married women like Tanya.

Mara's reality was her life in D.C. and taking care of her mother. That was what she needed to focus on, not falling for a man who was incapable of any true feelings.

When they got home, Zander excused himself, heading straight for his library. She knew he was upset at her, but it was better than her making a damn fool of herself over him. As long as she stayed focused, she would be fine. There was no denying the sexual attraction between then, and it would remain just that—an attraction.

Mara took a long, warm shower. She needed to keep things in prospective and she would be fine. Zander Tuskcan was just summer fun; she did not need to fall for him. Wrapped in a robe, Mara walked out of the bathroom to find Zander in the middle of her room, staring at the sketch Stone had done of her.

"What do you think?" She walked over to him.

He looked at her with hard, cold eyes. "When did he do this?"

"You don't like it?" Mara asked. Once again, cold eyes turned on her.

"You posed for him?"

Mara didn't know what to say.

"He saw you naked?" He looked at her for an answer.

Mara didn't expect him to react this way. The fact that Stone had seen her naked really upset him. Stone was an artist, so why should that bother him? Mara wondered how he'd react if he found out what had really happened between her and Stone. A sense of guilt suddenly washed over her as he turned and stormed out.

The evening was still bright enough for her to sketch, so Mara grabbed her pad and headed out to the pool. She was working on a new chair when she sensed someone watching her. She looked up to see Zander. He had showered and changed into a cotton T-shirt and sweat bottoms; his hair was still damp. He walked over and sat at her side, his eyes searching her face. She knew she could fall for him so easily, but she wouldn't. She couldn't.

"What?"

"You reminded me of my mother when she used to sit out here and sketch." His statement surprised her.

"I do?"

"Yes, she would sit right where you're sitting. I used to watch her as she worked on a piece." He looked at her sketchpad. "May I?" She gave it to him and watched as he flipped through the pages.

"So you like my designs?"

"They're amazing. Why didn't you pursue art?"

"I couldn't. Not if I wanted to eat or take care of my mother."

"So that explains the computer science degree."

"You got it."

He looked at her work again. "You're good." He continued to flip through her sketches.

"Thank you." She smiled at him.

"It's a shame to waste so much talent." The way he looked at her made her want to tell him everything. But she still had to be on her guard. He was complicated and intoxicating, a bad coordination.

"Computers are the future—I can't go wrong with it."

He studied her before responding. "That sounds like someone else's dream."

"I always liked computers so it was a logical choice. I also knew it would be the next-best means of taking care of my mother."

"Can I ask where your father is?"

Mara didn't like to talk about her father much. He was a distant memory. "He left us when I was only six. A few years ago we heard he died."

"Sorry to hear that." His voice softened.

"It's no big deal. It wasn't as if I really knew him."

"I see."

"You know if you ever want to go into business manufacturing these chairs, I could set up your company for you."

She shrugged. "I already have a career to look forward to in D.C."

"You really should think about this—you're very talented," he insisted.

"It would disappoint my mother."

"You do everything to please your mother?"

"Just about," she admitted.

"What about pleasing you?" His voice lowered to a sultry tone.

"I know how to please myself," she whispered.

His eyes filled with desire as he leaned into her. His mouth touched her neck gently as he placed small kisses there. She shivered and moaned as he kissed her ear. Why couldn't she resist him? His tongue caressed her skin and her toes curled. That was why she wanted him too much.

"I thought you were mad at me," she managed to get out between breaths. A hand covered her left breast, rubbing gently. He was making her wet. She laced her fingers through his damp hair.

"I can't stay away from you," he whispered. She shivered as her heart raced at his admission.

Mara closed her eyes as he covered her mouth with his. She returned his kiss with immense passion as his tongue found its way inside her mouth. She wrapped her arms around his neck, savoring the taste of him as his fresh musk scent filled her senses. She could kiss him forever. She slid her hands down to his back.

The sound of someone clearing his or her throat startled her. She pushed Zander away to see Shari and Patrick looking at them. Shari had a huge smile on her face. Patrick looked on with a surprised grin. She suddenly felt like a child getting caught with her hand in the cookie jar. Only her hands were all over Zander.

Mara jumped to her feet.

"Sorry for interrupting," Patrick grinned.

Mara looked at Zander. He didn't even look embarrassed that they were caught kissing.

"I'm glad you're here," Zander told Patrick. "There's some business we need to discuss."

Zander gazed back at her and gave her a sexy wink that made her smile as he took Patrick inside.

"What was that?" Shari asked, excited.

"What?" Mara asked innocently.

"How long has this been going on? I thought you were my best friend." Shari's eyes danced with intrigue. "You're supposed to tell me everything."

"Not everything." Mara cocked a brow at her. She was not about to go into detail with Shari about Zander. She just didn't think it was right.

"Yes, everything," Shari insisted.

Mara grinned and sat down. Shari sat beside her, excited and ready to hear more.

"OK, we slept together," Mara admitted.

"And?" Shari beamed.

"We had sex. That was it."

"So how do you feel about it?"

"You playing shrink now?"

"Come on, Mara, give me something, some glimmer of hope."

"Hope?" Mara was surprised by her choice of words.

"Yeah, for you and Zander to be together."

"Wow. Hold up—you wanted this?"

"Sure, why not. I knew you two would be great together."

"I don't think so. I mean, the sex is to die for, but I'm not about to fool myself with your brother. Plus, I'm on vacation—remember?"

"If it works out, you could just stay."

Mara laughed nervously. "And do what? I have a

life and a mother in D.C., Shari. You know I can't stay here. Plus, what would I do here?"

"Same thing you'd do in D.C."

"My mother's in D.C. D.C. is where I belong, not here in this fancy mansion playing Cinderella."

Shari looked at her, offended.

"I'm sorry, but I'm just being realistic. Yes, your brother and I slept together, but I'm not about to fool myself. I'm not in your league and I never will be."

"We're no different, Mara, and you know that."

"I love you, Shari, but I could never be like you or Tanya because I don't come from money and I don't have the breeding to fit into your society. As much as I'm loving all this right now, it's not me."

"My money didn't stop us from being friends, so why should it stop you from being with Zander?"

"Zander and I are not in love," Mara told her, hoping she'd drop the subject.

"Then why sleep with him? I know you, Mara. You don't sleep with anyone that you don't have feelings for."

"There's always a first time for everything," she shrugged.

"Don't lie to me and don't lie to yourself."

"I don't want to talk about it," Mara said. "By the way, Raven and Luc wanted to know when you were coming to visit."

"You've met them?"

"Zander and I had lunch with them earlier, but I met them at the fund-raiser where Tanya threw wine on me."

"She did what?" Shari said, shocked.

"Don't worry, I got her good when she came at me in the bathroom when she saw Zander kissing me."

"Zander kissed you in the bathroom? Back up and tell me what happened."

Mara told her the whole story. Shari stared at her in awe when she was done.

"So you had some night."

"You could say that." Mara smiled, remembering how it ended with her in Zander's arms. That was definitely the best part of the night. "So how's it going with Patrick?"

"Better than I expected," she beamed.

"So did you talk to him?"

Shari's face fell. "He told me that he did have an affair, but that it only lasted a few months."

"And he's been faithful to you since?"

"That's what he said."

"You don't believe him?"

"I don't know what to believe."

"Did you tell him about your affair?"

"I couldn't bring myself to tell him. I don't want to hurt him."

"Were you hurt when he told you the truth?"

"A little. A part of me knew he had an affair so I was kind of prepared for it. The first six months I was in D.C., I refused to talk to him. I didn't want to hear anything he had to say. Then he just showed up on campus one day and we were back on." The gleam in Shari's eyes told her that they had had one hell of a reunion. "So how was it?" Shari asked, switching the subject.

"That's nasty. Don't ask me about your brother." Mara pretended to be disgusted.

"I'm going to take that to mean he didn't disappoint you?"

"That man could never disappoint any woman." Mara sighed deeply.

"You're hooked."

"No, I'm not."

"I have never seen that look in your eyes before. Not once."

"Zander is . . . magnificent. I wish I could bottle him and take him home when I leave."

Shari looked at her, disappointed again.

"What?"

"Nothing," Shari said and frowned.

Mara was flattered that Shari thought she and Zander would get together, but of course she knew nothing would come of it. If anything, this was just a summer fling.

Helen was busy making dinner. Zander and Patrick were still locked up in the library. Mara showered and changed into a long linen sheath dress.

When she came back down, dinner was ready and Shari was helping to set the table while Helen talked proudly about her grandson. Zander and Patrick joined them in the kitchen and everyone sat down to dinner. They talked and laughed like a family. As Mara listened to the family stories, she thought of her mother, alone in D.C. without her.

"Mara, you OK?" Zander asked, rubbing the back of her neck. She gazed at him and tried to smile, but all she could think of was her mother.

"I need to call my mother—excuse me," she said, and quickly left the table. She ran to her room, where she threw herself across the bed and willed herself not to cry. Ever since she had been here she'd been an emotional wreck. She was always way too busy in D.C. to be this emotional.

Zander gently eased Mara's bedroom door open. She was on the bed, her face buried in her arms. He knew she was missing her mother, which was natural. He just hated the sad look in her eyes at the dinner table. He moved over to her and sat down and started rubbing her back. She didn't move or look at him. He heard her sniffle and he knew she was crying.

"Mara." He gently said her name, and she turned over onto her back, looking up at him. Her eyes were red from crying. Tears stained her cheeks.

"Did you call your mother?" he asked gently as she wiped her tears, sniffling.

"Not yet."

"Do you want me to go?"

"No." She threw her arms around his neck, bursting into more tears. He held her while she cried. His heart bled for her.

"Tell you what. Why don't you call your mother and I'll check on you later."

He kissed her briefly before leaving her alone.

Shari was pacing the hallway when Zander came out of Mara's room.

"Is she OK?" Shari asked, worried.

"She's fine," he reassured her.

"I didn't think she'd miss her that much. They're so close—maybe I shouldn't have forced her to come here."

"If you hadn't done that, then I wouldn't have gotten the chance to know her."

Shari smiled at him. "You do know I was hoping you two would hit it off."

"We did," Zander admitted, and Shari grinned widely at him. Zander pulled his sister into his arms, hugging her tight as she laughed.

"Zander, don't let her go," Shari said as he tucked her hair behind her left ear.

"I can't stop her if she wants to." Nothing had scared him since his parents' death. Now here he was, scared of losing a woman he had just met.

"You can't afford to let her go," Shari said.

Zander looked at his sister, finally understanding her motives. "Is that why you brought her here?"

"What do *you* think?" Shari told him and walked away. Zander's thoughts raced with the possibility of getting Mara to stay with him. She was so focused on returning to D.C. It was impossible. He just didn't see a way of getting her to stay.

Her mother answered the phone on the third ring, laughing. "Hello?"

"Mama?"

"Mara, are yu' OK?" She could hear the worry in her mother's voice.

"Yes, I'm fine." She heard a male voice ask her mother where the Dustbuster was. "Who's there with you?"

"It under de' sink," her mother called out.

"Mama, who's there with you?"

"Henry."

"Mr. Johnson?"

"Yu' sound different, yu' sure yu' OK?"

"Yeah, I'm fine."

"Yu' don't sound fine. Are yu' enjoyin' yu'self?"

"I miss you," Mara moaned into the phone.

"I miss yu', too, baby," Janice said. "Tell me what wrong now?"

"I was just worried about you."

"Yu' sure yu' OK?" Mara wanted to tell her everything but she couldn't.

"Yeah, how's work?"

"Can't wait to go on vacation."

"When does your vacation start again?"

"Next week."

"So where are you and your church group going this time?" Mara asked. Last year the church group had gone on a weekend outing in Virginia.

"Henry says it's a surprise."

"Henry?" Mara asked, alarmed. "What's going on with you and Henry?"

"Nothing."

"You're sure?" she pressed.

"Yes, Mama," her mother said and Mara laughed, lightening the mood considerably. They talked for another ten minutes before she got off the phone. She felt a lot better. There was a brief knock and Shari entered, a worried look on her face.

"You OK?"

"Yeah."

"You are not supposed to be sad while you're on

vacation. This is not what Janice wanted," she scolded playfully.

"I know—I'm just not used to being away from her," she whispered.

"And what's going to happen when you get married?"

Mara looked at her, stumped. "She comes along," Mara told her. She just couldn't see not having her mother with her.

"And if she doesn't want to come along?"

"Why wouldn't she?" She had never thought of ever leaving her mother. They had been together forever and it would always be like that.

"Mara, maybe it's time you started living your own life. You seem to think your mother can't do without you, but I'd say she's been doing just fine since you've been gone, don't you?"

Then it came to her. "Mr. Johnson?"

"I happen to know that he's very fond of your mother."

"No!"

"Your mother is a very attractive woman, and she sure ain't dead, so why wouldn't he be interested in her? He's a man, isn't he?"

Mara had to sit down. She couldn't believe it. How come she hadn't seen it? Sure, they spent a lot of time together. Henry was always fixing something in the apartment and he was always there for Sunday dinner. Apparently he was there for a lot more. How could they keep it from her?

"She said he was just her church brother."

"Because she knows how protective you are of her."

"How long have you known this?"

"Almost a year."

"A year!" Mara jumped to her feet and headed straight for the phone. Shari snatched the phone from her and hung it up.

"Janice is a grown woman, and she's living her life. You should do the same," Shari said and walked out of the room. Stunned, Mara sat on the bed trying to process it all.

Her mother had a man, and he'd been right under her nose all this time, but Mara hadn't seen it. She couldn't wait to get back to D.C. to give her mother a piece of her mind. How could she keep something like this from her and for so long?

Unable to sleep, she left her room. She didn't want to be alone. She needed Zander. His door was ajar and she quietly entered. He was reading in bed. He put his book away and held his hand out to her. She practically ran over to him. She got in under the covers beside him, wrapping her arms around his waist. She rested her head on his chest. He held her to him.

"You OK?"

She nodded, closing her eyes. He reached for the light, turned it off, and repositioned himself, cradling her in his arms. She fell asleep, secure in his arms.

Chapter 17

Mara really wasn't in the mood for a party but Shari insisted on it. She was distracted with thoughts of Henry and her mother together. Granted, Henry was a good man. The fact that her mother had hidden the affair from her bothered her. Was she that protective of her mother? And even if she was, her mother still didn't have to hide it from her.

And to make matters worse, she was starting to miss Zander. He had left on a business trip two days ago. She knew she shouldn't be missing him, but she couldn't help it. She loved being with him and she couldn't wait to see him, to kiss him and feel his hands on her body. She sighed, frustrated, as she became aroused at the thought of him inside her. She recalled their first time together and smiled with pleasant memories. What the hell had he done to her?

As Mara made her way downstairs, the front door opened and Zander walked in. Her heart raced at the sight of him. He looked tired, but oh so good. She continued down the stairs, not taking her eyes off him. He looked up then, seeing her, and returned her stare. She stopped at the bottom of the stairs a few feet away from him. He slowly looked her over. His dark eyes glowed with desire.

"Beautiful," he whispered. She smiled and turned around, giving him a better look at her short red dress with its flowing skirt. She wore high-heeled mules that flattered her legs.

"You like?" she asked softly, covering the distance between them.

"Very much," he said. "I don't think I should let you go around looking this good. Some man might want to steal you from me."

"I don't think so," she teased, tracing a finger over his bottom lip. "I'd kiss you, but I'd have to redo my lipstick."

He pulled her to him and lowered his head. She reached up for his kiss. It felt good to be in his arms.

"Enough, you two!" Shari's voice startled them. "You let go of her, or you'll ruin her makeup. And you, Mara, behave!" Shari pulled her away from Zander. Mara pouted, disappointed.

"I'll be waiting," Zander whispered in her ear, sending shivers down her spine. Mara watched him as he headed toward his library. She couldn't wait to get back here. The thought of being with him pleased her greatly. She looked at Shari to find her shaking her head.

"I'm ready. Let's go." She took Shari's arm, rushing toward the front door. Shari giggled.

"So what is this dinner party about?" Mara asked in the car. She really didn't want to go to a dinner, not with Zander home alone, wanting her.

"It's a surprise party for Patrick, actually."

"Oh?"

"You'd rather be with Zander?" Mara couldn't help the smile that surfaced as she recalled the desire in his eyes. "I thought my brother didn't mean anything to you. Now, all of a sudden, you can't be without him . . . Hmmm, this is interesting."

"I'm not even going to talk about it," Mara said sternly, hoping she'd drop the subject.

"Why not? You like him, don't you?"

"Yes."

"You love him?"

Mara stared at her, stunned.

"I'm not in love with your brother," Mara insisted. She couldn't afford to fall for a man like Zander. He wasn't capable of truly loving any woman. If she thought he could love her, she was kidding herself. He didn't believe in love—he had said it himself. So she wasn't about to think differently about him, just because Shari wanted them together.

"Why don't you look me in the eyes and tell me that one again? You have spent more time with him than I have. To tell you the truth, this is the first time that Zander has ever paid this much attention to any woman. What exactly does that say to you?"

Mara looked at her. "It's not going to happen, Shari. As much as you want it to . . . Zander and I are just having fun. That's all."

"Are you trying to convince me or yourself?"

Just then the car came to a stop, and Mara was thankful it did.

Patrick was very surprised when he walked into

his mother's living room and realized the party was for him. He couldn't stop kissing Shari. Mara was thankful that Patrick kept Shari away from her with her lingering questions about how she felt about Zander. She couldn't allow herself to feel too much or she'd only end up seriously hurt.

Franklin was there, and, of course, he was by her side all night, talking her ear off about his new girlfriend. Mara welcomed the distraction. Until Zander walked into the room and headed straight for her. The look on his face said he wasn't staying, and neither was she. Excitement raced through her, making her wet.

"Say good-bye," he whispered as he caressed her ear with his lips. She shivered as her nipples hardened. "You have five minutes to meet me out front." He turned and walked out. She let out a long breath and licked her lips. She couldn't wait to be in his arms.

Mara found Franklin and asked him to inform Shari of her departure. Minutes later, she climbed into the passenger seat of Zander's Jaguar. Instantly he took off before she could clip in her seat belt.

"What's the hurry?" she asked, intrigued, with a smile.

"You'll see once I get you home." He sped off.

At the house, Zander led her into his library. The entire room was illuminated with large candles. She gasped in awe at the setting in the middle of the room: a blanket with pillows and a platter with fruit and a bottle of red wine.

"For me?" She was truly flattered.

He closed the door and moved up behind her, wrapping his arms around her waist and pressing his lips into her neck. Mara tingled at his touch as she leaned back into him.

"I missed you," he said. His warm lips caressed her neck, sending tingles exploding under her skin.

Mara grasped his hands and bought them to her breasts. His fingers massaged her. She loved his gentle touch. He knew exactly how to touch to warm her to the core. She turned slowly to look at him. His eyes told her everything, especially his need for her. His hands moved down to her rear and he brought her closer to him. They undressed each other with exploring hands. He lowered her onto the blanket and covered her body with his. His kisses were hot and sweet, bringing her body and soul alive. She couldn't get enough of him, he was so addictive. He slowly moved down her body, pushing her legs apart. His hands and mouth explored her inner thighs, causing her senses to spin out of control.

He buried his head between her legs and kissed her gently. Stars exploded in Mara's head. She moaned his name over and over again as the light, teasing kisses left her breathless. Then his mouth engulfed her in a sensuous assault, his tongue setting off an orgasm that left her quivering and senseless.

His mouth trailed a hot path back up her body as he settled between her legs. He reached for a condom, and she watched him put it on. She liked

watching him. Mara welcomed Zander, as he slowly
and luxuriously entered her. She moaned his name
as she wrapped her arms and legs around him. She
didn't want to ever be separated from him. They
were so perfect together, moving against each other
in perfect union. Mara raked her fingers through his
hair, kissing him deeply. She cried out his name as
her body exploded in pure pleasure. She felt him
surge against her and held on tighter.

An hour later, they lay naked in each other's
arms.

Zander kissed her lips. "I didn't think I'd missed
you so much."

She ran her fingers through his hair, tucking it
behind his ears. "I missed you, too."

"God, you're so beautiful." He kissed her eyes one
at a time. She gazed at him, wondering if he was for
real. This was the kind of man every woman dreamt
of. She had him, yet she knew it wouldn't last.

"What are you thinking about?" he asked, caressing her breasts.

"How much I'm going to miss you when I go
back to D.C.," she said, and felt his body stiffen
against her. She regretted her words. Silently, she
swore. She hadn't meant to say it like that. For the
first time since she met him, she saw hurt surface
in his eyes and it tore at her heart. She never
meant to hurt him. He had been so wonderful to
her. She eased him onto his back and climbed on
top of him, kissing him gently. He quickly responded, wrapping his arms around her. It was
the only way she knew how to say she was sorry.
Sorry for all that was to come, especially when it
would end with Shari's wedding.

* * *

Zander held Mara close to him as she slept. He felt hopeless and afraid. Afraid he would lose her. He wanted her to stay here with him. He wanted to get to know her better. He didn't want her to go back to D.C., but he didn't know how to ask her to stay. And even if he did, he knew she wouldn't because all she talked about was going back to D.C. For the second time in his life since his parents' deaths, he had no control over his emotions. He could do nothing but hold her close. He didn't want to ever let her go. He would just have to savor the time they had together. After she had fallen asleep, he picked her up and carried her upstairs to her room. He placed her under the covers and watched her sleep, memorizing her features. He kissed her lightly and left.

Chapter 18

When Mara woke the next morning she found a note on her pillow; it read: *"I'll be in NYC for the next few days. Zander."*

Zander had left her a note. He didn't have to, but he had. She was flattered. After a quick shower, Mara went down for breakfast. Helen had just placed strips of bacon on a paper towel. She greeted Helen as she poured herself a cup of coffee. She munched on a strip of bacon as she added cream to her coffee.

"Slept well?" Helen asked, sitting down with her own cup of coffee.

"Yes, thank you." Mara smiled at her, reaching for another strip of bacon. Shari came rushing into the room, excited.

"Guess what?" Her eyes danced with glee.

"What?" Mara asked, curious.

"Zander called. He wants you to join him in Manhattan."

Mara paused with her cup at her mouth. "What?"

"You should go. You'll have fun," Helen said and smiled. Mara looked at Helen. Helen nodded with a knowing smile. Did she know about her and Zander? Obviously she did and was pleased with it. Had Shari told her?

"Come on, I have to help you pack," Shari said, and Mara turned her attention to her. "I know he's going to take you to the theater, so let's make sure you have the proper attire."

Zander's request came as a surprise. She had to admit that the idea of going to New York City was exciting. She had heard a lot about Manhattan, and she was looking forward to seeing it. Of course, seeing Zander was the icing on her cake.

Mara sat watching Shari as she picked out a few dresses that were a must for her evenings in the city. Mara found it all amusing, watching Shari fuss over the clothes. One would think Shari was the one going to New York City to be with her man. Mara packed her toiletries while she listened to Shari rattle on about places she must see in Manhattan. Getting to all those places in a weekend was impossible, but it was fun seeing Shari so excited.

An hour later, Shari hugged her, all misty-eyed, as she was about to get into the car.

"Make sure he takes you to . . ."

"Enough!" Mara told her, and Shari nodded her understanding.

"Have fun!" Shari called to her.

"I will," she laughed, getting into the car.

It was almost a two-hour drive into the city. The skyline was spectacular. Mara loved it as the car made its way through downtown Manhattan, the streets bustling with life. The driver assisted her out of the car on Park Avenue overlooking Central Park. She was in one of the wealthiest areas of the city, and it showed with its impressive apartment buildings and uniformed doormen. The driver got her bags and directed her into the lobby of a building.

The driver stopped at the reception desk and told the clerk that Mara was here for Mr. Tuskcan. The clerk got a key from a box behind him and handed it to Mara.

"Tenth floor, room 1005."

Mara thanked him and headed toward the elevators with the driver in tow. The golden-toned lobby was magnificent, illuminated by a large glass chandelier. On her way up on the elevator, a small white lady and her dog got on, and Mara could have sworn the woman and the dog looked alike. The thought made her smile and the old woman smiled back at her, as she discreetly looked Mara over.

Zander's apartment was a luxury spread, with parquet floors, modern furnishings, and a spectacular view. It overlooked the park and the skyscrapers in the misty skylines of New York City.

Mara made herself at home, checking out the three-bedroom, two-bath complex with its fully equipped kitchen. In the refrigerator she found fresh fruit salad. She took a small bowl and went back out onto the patio to enjoy the scenery.

"Mara?" She heard her name, and a tingle went down her spine. It was Zander, and he was calling for her. "Mara, you here?" he called out again. Mara rushed inside to find him coming into the kitchen. He smiled at seeing her. She ran to him and jumped into his arms and wrapped her legs and arms around him. He kissed her deeply, squeezing her to his hard body. He smelled wonderful. He felt wonderful. She had hungered for him for so long. She pulled his hair loose. She could so easily get used to this man. She could fall for him so easily, but she wouldn't. She would simply enjoy whatever time she had with him.

"I didn't think you'd come," he said, setting her down on the kitchen counter. Mara fingered his hair and caressed his prickly cheek, looking deeply into his eyes. She still couldn't get over how handsome he was and that he wanted her here with him.

"Are you kidding? I've never been to New York City before. I'm so looking forward to all this."

"Is that all you're looking forward to?" He caressed her thighs. She grew even warmer under his touch. He had skillful hands, hands that with a single touch could make her melt.

"Hell, no."

He laughed and kissed her briefly. "Good. I hope you're ready for tonight."

"What are we doing?" She was excited and she couldn't help it.

"I have tickets to *Chicago*. We only have an hour before the show. I was hoping to be here earlier to take you to dinner, but . . ."

"I'm not hungry, at least not for food." She cut him off, giving him a sultry look.

"We don't have time," he warned. She pouted in disappointment. "What am I going to do with you?" He smiled.

"Anything you want," she told him seductively.

"Go get ready," he demanded gently. She pouted and sauntered off, throwing him a steamy look in the process.

Twenty minutes later, Mara emerged in a black scoop-neck chiffon dress, with strappy sandals and a matching purse. Zander came out of his room a few minutes later in evening slacks, a matching jacket, and a mock necktie. He hadn't shaved and his hair was loose. He looked so damn good.

"Don't look at me like that." He moved over to her.

"And why not?"

"We might not leave this room."

"Sounds good to me."

"I want to show you Manhattan."

"And I want to show you . . ."

"Mara!" he warned, smiling.

"OK, I will behave," she cooed seductively.

"Good, now come along. It's bad enough you look so damn good."

"Thank you," she said and blushed.

Traffic was crazy in Manhattan. Mara enjoyed the sights as they made their way into Times Square. They got to the theater about ten minutes before curtain time. As Zander ushered her into the Shubert Theatre, Mara was fascinated by the intricate design on the walls.

Chicago was by far the most entertaining musical Mara had ever seen and she enjoyed every minute of it. After the show, Zander took her to the Tavern on the Green for a late, light dinner and drinks. By the time they got back to the apartment it was after one A.M. They were both dead tired and fell asleep in each other's arms in the master bedroom, still dressed.

Mara woke the next morning to find Zander gone. She also found a note on the pillow saying he had gone out for muffins. Mara decided to take a shower. She came out of the shower in a robe, and the scent of fresh coffee invaded her senses. She ventured into the kitchen to find Zander arranging the biggest muffins she had ever seen on a plate. Coffee was brewing.

"Morning." She sauntered over to him.

He pulled her into his arms, kissing her deeply. "Morning—did you sleep OK?" He caressed her cheek.

"Yes."

He kissed her neck. She tingled all over as his warm lips explored her neck. He reluctantly pulled away to pour her a cup of coffee. She was glad to have him like this.

"So what's on for today?" Mara asked, chewing on a piece of banana nut muffin.

"Wear comfortable shoes."

Dressed in a fitted white shirt and black capri pants with flat mules, Mara was ready to see New York City. Zander was also comfortable, dressed in blue jeans and a polo shirt.

A car waited for them outside. Mara enjoyed the busy sights of the city as they made it down Park Avenue. Their first stop was at Tiffany's on Fifth Avenue and Fifty-seventh Street.

"What do you think?" Zander asked Mara as they

looked at Tiffany's signature platinum-and-diamond stud earrings and matching diamond solitaire necklace.

"Shari will love it."

"I also had something else in mind for Shari." Zander pulled out his wallet and handed the saleslady his credit card. "I also want the pearls," he told the lady.

"Will you be taking them with you, sir?" The saleslady asked with a smile.

"No, I want them delivered to this address." He handed the saleslady a business card.

They left Tiffany's and headed for Chelsea Piers, where they went out on a small, private yacht that took them around Manhattan. Mara stood on deck, Zander at her back, as he pointed out the Brooklyn and Manhattan bridges to her. The empty spot where the World Trade Towers used to be. The yacht also took them to the Statue of Liberty and past Ellis Island. They had lunch at a restaurant at Chelsea Piers before heading back to the apartment, where they showered and took a nap together.

Around seven they got dressed and went to dinner at a restaurant in midtown named Flares, which specialized in seafood and sushi. Mara wasn't up to the raw fish, so they both had roasted sea bass on a bed of spinach and baby vegetables served with dry white wine. After dinner, Zander took her to Times Square, where Mara admired the bright lights, big screens, and billboards. Hand in hand, they strolled through the busy streets filled with New Yorkers and tourists.

"Want to go to a birthday party?" Zander asked as

they waited for a light to change on Forty-third Street.

"Whose birthday is it?"

"A business associate of mine. I told him I might stop by."

"Do we have to change?"

"No." Zander smiled at her, hugging her close to him. The party turned out to be at the Russian Tea Room on Fifty-seventh Street and was in full swing when they got there. Mara found herself bobbing her head to the latest R&B music. A waiter approached then and Zander took two white wines off the tray, handing her one.

"He knows his music," Mara said as she bobbed to the latest R. Kelly tune.

"Zander, my man." Mara turned to see a large, handsome African-American man coming toward them. He embraced Zander warmly. "I thought your stiff behind wasn't coming."

"Hey," Zander responded, amused.

"Who's the fine lady?" he asked, taking her hand and kissing the back of it, while pulling her toward him.

"Hey, she's mine," Zander told him and pulled her back to him. "Mara Evans, this is Lee Brown, a good friend if he stays away from my woman."

Mara smiled at his playful possessiveness.

"Nice to meet you, Lee, and happy birthday."

Lee winked at her, playfully. "Thank you, beautiful. So you're the lovely who's been keeping him captive." Lee's eyes gleamed with mischief. Zander actually looked guilty as Lee slapped Zander on the back, laughing.

"Enjoy the party. There's plenty of food and

drinks, and save me a dance, beautiful." He winked at her again before walking off.

The party was great, and Mara was introduced to a number of Zander's associates. Lee found them an hour later and dragged Mara out onto the floor for a dance. He moved well for a man of his height. Of course, Mara matched his moves. Halfway into the second dance, Zander came for her, cutting in on Lee.

"So you had fun?" Zander asked as they entered the apartment a little after four.

"Oh, yes."

"Good. I'm glad you did."

He looked at her and Mara moved into his arms, kissing him deeply. She pulled at his clothes, never breaking their kiss. He helped her undress him. Mara stood back, looking at his beautiful naked body. She would never forget him. She slowly started to undress before him. He didn't move. His hungry eyes watched her every move. She moved up to him, running her hands over his chest and arms, loving the feel of him. He reached down and lifted her into his arms, then took her into the bedroom where he placed her on the bed. She held her hands out to him as he joined her, then pulled him to her, kissing and caressing him. He moved away briefly reaching for a condom on the nightstand. He quickly put it on and rejoined her. She accepted him with all pleasure. Her senses escalated with the feel of him inside her. She held him close, never wanting to let go, yet knowing she would have to. But for now, he was all hers.

* * *

Sunday morning, Mara woke in Zander's arms. She smiled and snuggled closer to him.

"You awake?"

"Yeah, so what's on the agenda for today?" she asked, looking into his eyes.

He looked at her sadly. "I have to fly to Atlanta."

"I thought we'd have today also." She couldn't hide her disappointment.

He kissed her gently, hugging her tightly.

"I'm sorry about this."

"How long will you be in Atlanta?" She wrapped her arms around him, pressing her ear into his chest, listening to his heartbeat.

"Two days."

"So I'll see you in two days?"

"You're taking this well."

"You have a business to run—I don't."

"Thanks for understanding." He kissed her again. "Let's go out for breakfast. There's a great little café a few blocks away."

An hour later they sat in the café over a healthy serving of homemade breakfast.

"I'm sorry I didn't bring you to Manhattan sooner."

"I had a great time from what I've seen so far."

"My father used to surprise my mother with weekend visits to the city. She loved it—the shopping, the sights."

"Shari told me you were with them when they died. That must have been hard for you." She watched as his eyes darkened with sadness. A part of her wished she hadn't bought it up.

"Yes. I was always away in boarding school. I was home for the summer and insisted on tagging along. I felt like I was losing them, and I wanted to get to know them again." He smiled softly. "We had a great summer. They took me everywhere. We were coming back from Atlantic City—I had just turned seventeen." He paused, swallowed hard, and took a sip of his coffee. "A semi truck swung over on us. I woke up in the hospital, and they were gone, just like that."

The pain in his voice was too real. Tears burned Mara's eyes. She reached over and took his hands into hers, caressing them gently. "It's OK." She whispered.

He cleared his throat. "It took me almost five years to be able to talk about it."

"The good thing is that you can," she said.

He looked at her as if seeing her for the first time. A small smile curved his lips. "If only you weren't leaving . . ." He stopped, as if catching himself.

"Let's not talk about that—let's just enjoy our time together."

He studied her for a moment. "Why are you so afraid of what's happening between us?"

"Please don't," she pleaded, swallowing her fears. He was asking too much of her.

"OK," he agreed reluctantly. Mara knew it wasn't the answer he wanted, but it was all she could give him at the moment. She had to be careful with him. It had been wonderful since she got here, but it was temporary.

They took a stroll after breakfast. Zander talked about the neighborhood as she took in the designs of the buildings. Back at the apartment, they packed their bags.

Mara was sitting in the living room watching TV when Zander emerged from his bedroom, talking on the phone.

"Tell you what. We'll talk when I get there. I have a plane to catch," he said into the phone.

Zander replaced the receiver and took the seat beside her, then took her hand, caressing it. She looked at him, unable to hide the sadness in her eyes. He kissed her gently. She sighed, savoring the taste of him. He pulled back, caressing her cheek.

"What are we doing?" she asked, suddenly afraid.

"Getting to know each other," he said with a smile.

"This is dangerous, Zander. I'm leaving soon and . . ." He kissed her, halting her words. She clung to him, not wanting to let go. She raked her fingers through his hair, deepening the kiss.

Eventually they parted, looking deeply into each other's eyes.

"Let's just enjoy this," he whispered.

"No strings, no regrets?" she said softly.

For what seemed like a lifetime, they simply stared at each other, both obviously afraid of what they were feeling.

"This is my cell number—call me late in the evening," Zander said, breaking the silence. He handed her his card. She took it, looking at the number he had circled. "It will be difficult to get me during the day."

She looked up at him longingly. Instantly he was

beside her, kissing her hungrily. She returned his kiss, pulling at his clothes.

"We don't have time," he whispered as he pulled her dress over her head, tossing it aside.

"I know," she said, breathless as he sucked his earlobes. He moaned, reaching for a condom—and then for her panties. Quickly all their clothes were gone and they were on the sofa naked, wrapped around each other. Zander entered her hard and fast, taking her breath away. Mara reached up to meet his every thrust, moaning his name and a couple of curse words in between as he drove hard into her core. She gripped his behind, biting into his shoulders. Her senses spun out of control as her body convulsed beneath him. She heard him moan deeply and felt his body jerk as he found his releases. Moments later, as they were trying to catch their breaths, the buzzer sounded.

"Damn it!" Zander cursed as he unwrapped his body from hers. Mara moaned in disappointment as he slid out of her. "That's for me—your car should be here in half an hour," Zander told her as he quickly put on his clothes. She watched him with a slight yet very satisfying smile on her face. He paused, looking down at her. His eyes flowed over her naked body. She loved the way he looked at her with such appreciation and interest.

"You are so wicked." He grinned, pulling on his shirt and turning away. She laughed.

"Get dressed," he demanded gently.

Chapter 19

"How was Manhattan?" Shari asked, excited. They were sitting in the kitchen.

"It was great," Mara exclaimed. "Really great." She grinned.

"I'm glad you two are getting along," Shari beamed.

"So what's going on with Patrick?"

"We talked."

"And?"

"He said he had a feeling I was with someone, but then he really couldn't blame me, knowing he had kept our coming marriage a secret."

"Thank God he's understanding."

"Yeah, but it still didn't make telling him any easier, but I had to."

"I know." Mara squeezed her hand in comfort.

Unable to sleep, Mara sat up in bed thinking about Zander and the time they had spent together. It was all so perfect, but it would soon end.

It would be foolish of her to even envision a future for her and Zander. They were good together physically; there was no denying the chemistry between them, but that was all it would be. They were from two different worlds, and she sure as hell didn't fit in here. It was fun pretending, but she would not fool herself about her situation. As much as she was attracted to Zander, she knew deep down he wasn't the man for her. Zander was by far the best lover she had ever had. The memories of them together made her moan. He would be hard to forget. Suddenly she needed to hear his voice. Picking up his card from her bed table, Mara dialed his number.

"Hello, Zander's line." Tanya's unmistakable voice came over the line. A dull feeling attacked Mara's entire being. She was so stunned she slammed down the phone without saying anything. He had gone to Atlanta to be with Tanya. She was such a fool! Sure he was enjoying their time together, while he was still enjoying Tanya. He had told her that it was over between him and Tanya. Apparently he had lied to her. It made Mara steaming mad. He had played her for a fool. How could she have been so stupid? Then again, what did she expect from a man like him? He had money and power. He could have any woman he wanted. Yes, she was flattered he wanted to be with her, but obviously it was only to play games. She had definitely learned a very valuable lesson. But she wasn't about to just let it go like that. The rebel in her couldn't let her.

Picking up the phone, she hit the redial button. Again, Tanya answered, breathless this time. She wondered if they were having sex. Mara felt disgusted as images of Zander and Tanya flashed before her. Her entire body tightened with anger.

"Let me talk to Zander," she demanded.

"We're busy right now," Tanya said. Mara closed her eyes as an unbearable pain tore through her heart. If Tanya had been in front of her, she knew she would tear her apart. But Tanya wasn't the only one to blame here.

"Put him on the phone!"

"How long did you think your little affair with him would last?" Tanya asked nastily. Her words stung deep. Mara felt like a fool.

"Let me talk to Zander," she demanded again.

"He's had enough of you, *ghetto girl*." Tanya's words were laced with nothing but hate. "Go home!" Tanya shouted.

Mara heard nothing but the dial tone. She stared at the phone, wanting to throw it across the room, but she didn't. She wanted to scream, but she bit her lips, forcing the scream back down. Tears welled in her eyes. God, she was stupid. He had played her for the fool that she was. She should have stuck to her plan and not gotten involved with him, but her hormones had taken over. Stupid, stupid, stupid!

Mara shook with such anger that she could barely breathe. She took deep breaths, focusing. What the hell could she do anyway? Nothing. Zander had set out to seduce her and he had done just that. She had no one to blame but herself. She had learned her lesson the hard way, a lesson she would never forget.

Mara woke with a killer headache. She felt like crap and she looked like it. Her eyes were red and

puffy from crying herself to sleep. She felt like a
fool, crying over Zander, but she wasn't able to
hold back the tears. She almost didn't want to go
downstairs to face Shari or Helen, but she was
hungry.

She found Helen in the kitchen making breakfast. She took one look at Mara and gasped.

"I know, I know," she moaned before Helen
could say anything.

"Are you OK?"

"Migraine," she answered, flinching as a sharp
pain raced through her temple.

"Let me get you some painkiller—does Advil
work for you?

"Yes, thank you."

Shari entered the kitchen. "Are you OK?" Shari
asked, concerned.

"Migraine and a rough night." She sipped her
coffee. Shari looked at her—there was more, but
Mara wasn't ready to talk just yet. She had to deal
with this in her own way. Helen handed her the
pills and Mara thanked her, swallowing them.

"Did Zander call?" Shari asked. Mara did her best
to keep her emotions off her face. An image of
Tanya and Zander together flashed before her eyes.
Mara closed her eyes and stilled her heart. What
was she doing to herself? He was nothing to her,
just a summer fling. Get over it!

"No," Helen answered.

Mara excused herself and went out to the pool.
She sat down, breathing deeply, trying not to think
of what he had done to her. It hurt like hell; it
shouldn't, but it did. She had fallen for him.

"Oh God," she moaned, putting her head down

on the table. She felt like crying. Getting involved with him was the biggest mistake of her life. She could blame no one but herself. She had played a dangerous game; she thought she was able to separate her feelings from the physical aspect, but she had failed.

"What's wrong?" Shari asked. Mara looked up at her.

"Nothing," she lied. She was going to miss Shari when she returned to D.C.

"Don't lie to me, Mara. I know when something's wrong."

"You are going to be Mrs. Rhone soon, and I probably won't see you after that."

"Oh, girl, don't say that. We'll always see each other."

"Maybe once a year at the most."

"Why don't you just stay here?"

"That's impossible."

Shari looked at her, dismayed. "I have to go out for a couple of hours. Want to come? It will cheer you up."

"I don't feel like it," she said and smiled softly.

"All right." Shari got up, disappointed. "I'll see you later."

"Thanks for understanding."

"We'll talk later." Shari gave her a comforting smile.

"OK." Mara managed a weak smile. She had always been able to talk to Shari about whatever ailed her, but this time she couldn't.

Not long after Shari left, Stone called and asked her to dinner. Mara accepted, needing the distraction. Stone was fun to be around, and she needed some cheering up right now. For her date with Stone, Mara wore a lavender sleeveless top with black slacks.

"Why are you going out with Stone?" Shari asked when she found Mara dressed and waiting for Stone's arrival.

"Because I want to."

"What about Zander?"

"What about him?" Mara couldn't hide her anger.

"What really happened between you two?"

"It doesn't matter anymore." Mara shrugged. "Zander and I are done. Which is a good thing, seeing that I leave soon anyway."

"I need to have a talk with my brother."

"As long as it's not about me."

Shari looked at her, confused.

"FYI, he's back with Tanya."

Shari was shocked. "What? What about you?"

"Like I said, it doesn't matter." She shrugged.

"I thought everything was fine with you two."

The doorbell chimed.

"I have to go."

Stone took her to dinner, then dancing. Mara enjoyed every minute of it, especially watching Stone getting his groove on the dance floor. Mara was so well entertained she didn't think of Zander until Stone was driving her home.

By the time Zander got home, he was tired. He had spent more time in Atlanta than he had planned, meeting with clients that demanded extra attention. His first priority was to get to the bottom of why Mara wasn't talking to him. He had misplaced his cell phone in Atlanta; of course, he had called the house, but she had refused to take his calls. They had had a great weekend in New York City. So what had changed since then? Why would she refuse to talk to him? It just didn't make any sense.

No one was home. Helen had left a note telling him she was at her daughter's house and would be back in the morning. Zander was tired, yet he couldn't sleep. He decided to review a few documents for the coming week in his library. He had gotten up to stretch when he noticed the time—it was after three. Where the hell were they? Helen hadn't mentioned anything about them staying at the Rhones'. So why weren't they home yet? He heard a car pulling up.

Mara turned to Stone as they came to a stop at the front door.

"Thanks for tonight." She smiled, gently.

"No. Thank you. You are always a pleasure to be around. Maybe I should find a way to trap you into staying in New Jersey. What do you think of me kidnapping you and forcing you to listen to all my corny jokes?"

Mara laughed and touched his cheek. "Your jokes are not corny. They could use some work, but they're certainly not corny."

Stone looked at her with wondering eyes. "I have to say good night," she told him.

He moved toward her; she turned her cheek to receive his kiss, but he cupped her face in his hands and his mouth covered hers. For a brief moment, she allowed him to kiss her. It didn't feel right. She pulled away, clearing her throat uncomfortably. All night he hadn't made one sexual move toward her. Being with him was like being with a great friend. She suddenly felt depressed.

"It's OK. I understand." He smiled.

"Do you really? I mean, I'd hate to think that I'm leading you on."

"You're not, trust me."

"Could you be any cooler?"

"Yes, if I had you, but your heart belongs to someone else. So I will suffer in silence." He winked, and she laughed.

"You are one classy guy, do you know that?" She smiled, relieved.

"Yes." He grinned with conceit.

"No wonder I like you."

"You do?" He pretended to be excited.

"Good night, Stone." She kissed his cheek, laughing. He beamed.

"Let's have lunch before you leave. I still want to see your sketches."

"OK."

Helen was making sandwiches for lunch when Mara finally made it downstairs at 11:30.

"Were you all right last night?" She handed Mara a sandwich and some coffee.

"I went dancing with Stone, actually." She took a bite of the sandwich.

"Oh," Helen said dryly. Mara wasn't even going to address the issue. It was over with her and Zander, and that was the end of it.

She noticed that Helen was also putting food on another plate.

"Shari's back?"

"No. Zander's home," Helen told her, looking right at her. So he was home. The anger came back, but she suppressed it.

Just then Zander walked in. Her eyes immediately went to him. He looked so good, dressed in slacks and a blue cotton shirt. His shirt was opened halfway, exposing that magnificent chest. Tanya's scent was probably lingering on him. Their eyes met, and held, and Mara was chilled with the coldness there. She looked away to find Helen's disappointed eyes on her. Zander said nothing as he got his coffee, picked up his plate, and walked right out of the room.

"What's going on with you two?" Helen asked.

"Nothing, which is the way it should have always been."

Helen gave her a strange look. Mara excused herself and went to her room to get the sketchpad.

Chapter 20

Mara was sketching by the pool when Shari joined her later that evening.

"Hey."

"Hey, you OK?" Mara asked her when she saw the frown on Shari's face.

Shari flopped down into the chair and let out a big sigh. "Yeah, except about what's going on with you and Zander. Helen just briefed me. So you two aren't even talking?"

"I really don't want to get into it."

"Why not?"

"Because I should have known better than to sleep with him. He's your brother, and you're my best friend. It was a bad call, but it's done and over."

"I just don't get it. You two had such a strong connection."

"Strong only in the physical sense."

"I've never seen Zander so alive since you got here. It has to be more than that."

"Shari, just let it go."

Shari was disappointed—she knew that. But Mara had made a terrible mistake, and that mistake was Zander. No regrets, no strings, she reminded herself, and hardened her heart.

* * *

Later that day, Mara learned that Zander had gone to Manhattan on business. A part of her was happy she didn't have to face him. It would give her time to put her emotions in order.

A few days later, Stone invited her to lunch at his studio. She accepted and took her sketches along for him to look at.

"These are magnificent," he commented. She beamed at his compliment. They were sitting in his workroom, which overlooked his private showroom. "You definitely chose the wrong career," he said in admiration. "How many of these have you done?"

"I've been sketching for over ten years. I have a box of books in D.C. with everything from clothes to accessories. The past few years I've been into chairs."

"You really are talented."

"Thanks."

"You should do something with these."

"That's what Zander said." She caught herself and stopped. She was done with Zander—she had to remember that.

"Something wrong?" Stone gazed at her, curious.

"No," she said, forcing a smile.

"You sure?"

"Yes."

Stone studied her closely. "It's Zander, isn't it?"

"Yes, and I don't want to talk about it."

Stone's phone rang as he was about to respond. Mara was glad it did. Stone excused himself to answer it. She was glad it ended that conversation.

She needed to stay focused, and not think of Zander. Stone returned with the phone and handed it to her.

"It's Shari."

Mara took the phone. "Hey, what's up?" she said into the phone. Stone started to clean up their lunch plates.

"I'm going to get my hair done," Shari said. "I could swing by and pick you up. You could use a touch-up, but if you're busy . . . ?" Mara knew she was trying to get her away from Stone.

Mara looked at Stone, who was now putting plates in the sink. He was a good man, but he wasn't for her. "No. Come get me."

"I'm ten minutes away," Shari sang. "See you in a bit."

Mara switched off the phone and moved to help Stone clean up. "Shari's coming for me—we're going to the hair salon."

"So when can we do this again?"

"Soon."

"Great." Stone smiled. Mara appreciated his understanding.

"How was lunch?" Shari asked the minute Mara got into the car.

"Good." She tossed her sketchpad on the back seat. Shari gazed back at her sketchpad.

"You showed Stone your sketches?"

"He thinks I wasted my time studying computers."

"I've been telling you that for years," Shari said. "You know, Zander had some really great ideas about your chairs. You should talk to him about it."

"I don't think so," Mara responded dryly. "Plus, I don't want anything to do with your brother—it's that simple," she snapped.

Shari looked surprised.

"I'm sorry."

"Don't be—I didn't know you hated him that much." Shari sounded hurt.

Mara sighed heavily. "I don't hate Zander. I don't know him well enough to hate him."

"Do you really intend to throw away your God-given talent?"

"No, I intend to use what I already have—my computer science degree—to take care of myself and my mother."

"Will you be happy doing that?"

"I have no choice but to be happy with it."

"And if you had the choice to make your chairs and be happy?" Shari looked at her as they waited for a light to change.

"Not in my world."

"It's not as difficult as you think." She smiled.

"In your world."

"Hey!"

"Sorry, but you know I don't have the luxury to pursue design. It's just a hobby—let's just leave it at that."

"Sometimes you have this one-sided view of things that gets on my nerves. Just thought you should know that."

"I know, but it's my reality."

"You always keep putting up this rich/poor wall between us, why? What's with that?"

"Like it's not real?"

"I could smack you," Shari said and sighed in frustration. Mara laughed. Shari slapped her hard on the thigh.

"Ouch!"

"You deserved that."

"I'm glad you're not mad at me."

"I could never be mad at you. Yes, you can be stubborn, but you are my best friend."

"Love-you-too."

"I just wished you and Zander . . ."

"Stop it!"

"OK. OK." Shari backed off.

Zander had been in Manhattan for almost a week. He had buried himself in his work, because he needed to cool off. However, he just couldn't get the image of Mara and Stone kissing out of his head. That night when he saw them, he wanted to go outside and confront Stone. But he simply turned away and headed back to his library. He didn't understand her. She had refused his calls—now he knew why. One minute she was his, the next she was in Stone's arms. He decided the best thing was to stay away from her and get his head straight. As hard as he tried, he couldn't stop seeing her in Stone's arms. The thought of her with him was killing him.

In a week Shari would be married and Mara would return to D.C. The thought of never seeing her again weighed heavily on his mind. Maybe it was for the best, her leaving. He could get back to his regular routine, to his life. He should have known she was nothing but trouble, with her big brown eyes, full, sexy lips, and those breasts. He moaned as his body reacted to his thoughts. He wanted her—he couldn't deny it—but it all seemed so impossible. He turned over and punched his pillow. The clock read four A.M.

Chapter 21

It was a week before Shari's wedding, and Mara was trying her best not to miss Zander. He had been in Manhattan for over a week. She hated the fact that she missed him, but he had made his choice. She told herself not to regret her brief relationship with him, but somehow she couldn't. He had hurt her in the worst way by lying. She could never forget that.

Not able to concentrate on her sketches, Mara decided to take a nap. She was heading upstairs when the doorbell rang. She decided to answer it. She opened the door to find her mother and Mr. Johnson smiling at her.

"Mama!"

"Surprise!" her mother sang, holding out her arms. Mara ran to her, hugging her and kissing her cheek. She inhaled her mother's familiar scent of Irish Spring soap and floral body spray.

"What ya'll doing here?"

"We got invited to de' weddin'," her mother said.

"Shari didn't tell me."

"It's a surprise," Mr. Johnson told her, moving to hug her.

"Come in, come in." She ushered them inside as the driver brought their bags in.

Helen entered the foyer, and Mara introduced everyone.

"I was expecting you two an hour ago," Helen said after the introductions were done.

"The plane was delayed because of rain in D.C.," Janice told Helen.

"You knew they were coming?" Mara asked, smiling.

Helen grinned. "Oh, yes."

"And you didn't tell me?"

"You weren't supposed to know," Helen said. She didn't care that they had kept her mother and Henry's visit a secret. She was just happy to have her mother with her.

"This is some house," Janice said, as Mara helped her unpack her carry-on case.

"Wait until you see the rest of it," Mara said.

"Yu' look different." Her mother paused, looking at her.

"How different?" Mara asked, a bit nervous.

"Relaxed."

"It has been fun being here." Mara did her best to sound cheerful, but she could see the concern surfacing in her mother's eyes.

"What's wrong?" Her mother sat beside her.

"Nothing," she said cheerfully.

Her mother didn't believe her. Mara could see it in her eyes.

"OK." Janice smiled and hugged her.

"So how long has this being going on?" Mara

asked both her mother and Henry as they sat close together, looking like the perfect couple. They were having a light lunch of grilled chicken and pasta. She watched them closely as they smiled at each other. She felt a tinge of jealousy, but in a good way. Her mother had found love, no doubt about it. Mara was happy for them. Too bad she couldn't be as happy.

"A while," her mother finally answered, smiling lovingly at Henry. Mara had never seen her mother so happy. Mara watched as Henry stroked her mother's hand.

"Shari told you?" Henry asked, looking at her.

"Yes, and ya'll didn't have to hide it from me."

"We didn't know how yu'd react," Janice said.

"I think it's wonderful," Mara said to her mother, then looked at Henry sternly. "And you better take good care of her or I'll come after you." Mara knew he would do nothing less.

"You know I'll take good care of her." Henry looked at her mother with those loving eyes and Mara knew then that he really did love her mother.

"Janice, Henry, you're here," Shari exclaimed, joining them. Shari hugged and kissed both Janice and Henry.

"Thanks for having us," Henry said.

"Are you kidding? You two have been so wonderful to me over the years. Of course I want you with me on my wedding day."

"You kept this from me." Mara poked Shari in the arm. Shari giggled.

"So you like my surprise?" Shari hugged her with a huge smile on her face.

"Hell, yes," she exclaimed, excited.

"Good. Henry, I got your tux—and Janice, I have a couple of dresses I picked up for you. I hope you like them."

"Oh, honey, thank yu'." Janice squeezed Shari's hand.

"I know it was kind of short notice."

"Don't worry about it—we're here, an' yu' goin' to have a wonderful weddin'," Janice said.

After lunch, Mara gave her mother and Henry a quick tour of the house.

Janice and Henry had afforded Mara the luxury of not thinking of Zander during the day as she caught up with them on what was happening in D.C. However, that night in bed alone, Zander was all she could think of. She should have never slept with him. If she hadn't, she wouldn't be in this state.

It was two A.M. and Mara was wide awake; she decided to get some of Zander's cognac to help her sleep. She knew he wasn't home, so it was safe for her to sneak a drink. She had poured some of the strong liquid and was about to walk out of the room when he walked in. She stopped in her tracks. Her heart raced at the sight of him. He looked tired, but so good. She stilled her heart, reining in her emotions. She watched him as his eyes devoured her body, then slowly returned to her face. She felt a heat creep into her as he looked at her with longing. She remembered hearing Tanya's voice on his phone and she went cold, moving toward the door. He slammed the door shut. She jumped, frightened by his sudden move. He was blocking her path, which forced her to stop a few feet away from him.

"Get out of my way," she demanded.

"Why didn't you take my calls?"

She stepped back and cocked her head and glared at him. Was he for real? After all he had done, he expected her to take his calls.

"Why should I?"

His jaw twitched rapidly. "You are truly trying my patience."

"Do I look like I care?" She rolled her eyes. His eyes narrowed and his lips tightened in anger. "Would you please move?" She reached for the doorknob. He grabbed her wrist. She gasped and dropped the glass. She cringed as the liquid splashed onto her bare feet. The glass hit the edge of the rug, but didn't break.

"Let me go!" she demanded, trying to pull free, but he held her tightly.

"Why are you doing this?"

"You should have considered that before you took me for a damn fool!" she snapped.

"What the hell are you talking about? You're the one that took me for a fool. The minute I turned my back, you're all over Stone," he snapped.

"What?"

"I saw you with him, kissing him!"

She was momentarily surprised by his words. "He kissed me, I didn't kiss him. And why is that any of your business?"

"Isn't it? Who the hell do you think you are to

be playing with me?" he asked in a tight, anger-laced voice.

"You started this game, remember?" she said coldly.

His eyes were hard as he glared at her. "So it's a game now? Is that what I am to you?"

"I just played the hand you dealt me," she responded coolly.

"What?" He looked at her, confused, but she wasn't buying it.

"I'm sorry I ever slept with you," she said through clenched teeth as she held her emotions in check. He released her instantly and stepped away from her. He looked devastated, but she didn't care. He had hurt her. "The only thing I don't regret about coming here is actually seeing Shari get married. Everything else has been a waste of my damn time." She walked away, her head held high. She wouldn't cry. She was finished crying over him.

Zander went numb at her harsh words. He couldn't move or think for a moment. Why was she doing this? She was blaming him for something he didn't know anything about. She needed to explain herself. She had used Stone to make him jealous. But why? He didn't understand her or where all this anger was coming from. They had made such passionate love, shared so much. How could she change so quickly? The hate in her eyes and her words was beyond belief. Someone or something had turned her against him. He thought of Stone, but he knew Stone wasn't the malicious type. Or was he? Her words had stung him to the core. He poured himself a glass of cognac, contemplating his next move.

Chapter 22

Mara woke up with a migraine the next morning from crying herself to sleep. She took two Advils and headed downstairs after making herself presentable. She didn't want her mother seeing her all broken up over some man. What she had done with Zander would be forgotten. She couldn't wait to get back to D.C., to her home, to her real life away from Zander.

Mara forced a smile to her face as she entered the kitchen moments later.

"Morning," she said.

Shari was on the phone, and smiled at her. Helen was shelling shrimp. Outside, she heard laughter and went to the door to see her mother and Henry frolicking in the pool like children. She got herself a cup of coffee and joined them poolside.

It was an absolutely gorgeous sunny day. Today was the day for a new beginning, she decided. Zander would no longer be of any concern to her. She had three days to go and she was counting every one of them.

Her mother and Henry got out of the pool and wrapped themselves in long terry cloth robes to join her at the table.

"I see you two are having fun."

"This is by far the best getaway I've ever been on," Henry said, smiling at Janice. It was amazing how a woman was when she was in love and that love was returned.

"Good morning," Zander said, joining them. He was dressed in a suit, obviously going to the office.

"Morning," Henry said, coming to his feet to shake Zander's hand.

"You must be Henry and Janice."

Zander smiled at them. Mara watched as her mother gave Zander the once-over, then smiled warmly at him. "Nice to meet you and thanks for joining us."

"Thank yu', Zander," her mother said with a smile as he shook her hand. He shook Henry's hand also, welcoming him.

Zander looked at Mara; she looked away. "Mara," he acknowledged her. She kept her eyes glued to her mug.

"Morning," she mumbled.

"I'm off to the office—I'll see you all later," he announced and walked away. Mara watched him, catching her breath and closing her eyes as the memories of being in his arms flooded her thoughts. She couldn't wait to go home so she could forget him.

"Nice-lookin' man," Janice commented with a smile. She rolled her eyes in disgust. "Yu' don't like him?"

"He's OK," she shrugged.

"Somethin' happened between yu' two?"

"No," Mara responded, much too quickly.

"I know when yu' lyin'."

Henry sat by, observing, saying nothing. Suddenly she wished he'd intervene. But he simply sat there listening to them.

"It's nothing."

"What'd he do?"

"Mama, I really don't want to talk about it."

"When yu' ready." Her mother patted her hand gently. Mara was glad her mother didn't press the issue.

Shari took them all to lunch, then for a bit of sightseeing. Janice loved the boutiques. Shari bought her mother an amber necklace and matching drop earrings. Henry got a Movado watch that Shari paid for before he could even object.

"Look at them," Mara commented as she and Shari sat on a park bench looking at her mother and Henry in the distance by a pond feeding the ducks.

Shari smiled. "They're happy together."

"I'm glad she has him."

"So does this mean that you aren't mad at them for keeping their relationship a secret from you?"

"Not when they are that happy."

"When are you going to tell me what's going on with you and Zander?" Shari asked.

"I know what you were trying to do with me and Zander, but we are too different. It was doomed from the start anyway. Sure, we had our fun, but it's over."

"Why?"

She wished she could tell her, but she just couldn't. "We are two mismatched people—it's as simple as that. Plus, sex alone doesn't make a relationship."

"I'm sorry to hear that," Shari said. "I thought it was more than that."

Mara didn't respond. She would never admit to Shari that it was more than that, at least it was for her, until Tanya answered his phone.

Janice's rich laughter drew her attention. Her mother seemed so much younger and so happy. At that moment Mara knew that was all that mattered to her.

Chapter 23

At the rehearsal for Shari's wedding, everyone was present except Zander. Helen told her he was in Atlanta. No doubt getting in his quality time with Tanya, Mara thought. Both Luc and Zander were to give Shari away; with Zander absent, they practiced without him.

Mara was the only one in Shari's bridal party. Franklin served as his brother's best man. Raven sang the most remarkable version of "I Will Always Love You," as Shari practiced walking down the aisle. Raven's singing range stunned Mara.

After the rehearsal they all adjourned to a French restaurant for dinner. Everyone was in a good mood and having a great time, except Mara. But she kept a smile on her face, determined that no one would know of her pain. This was a happy time for Shari, and she wouldn't ruin it by breaking down over a man she intended to forget in a few days.

She managed to escape into the garden for some fresh air. It was cool and clear. The stillness of the night and the chirping of the crickets were welcoming. She filled her lungs with the fresh night air.

"Hey, you OK?" Shari asked, coming up to her,

wrapping her arms about her waist. She leaned against her. They smiled sadly at each other.

"I'm gonna miss you so much."

"I'm gonna miss you, too, but it's not like you can't come visit me or me you," Shari said.

"I know, but it's not going to be the same."

"I know," Shari sadly admitted.

The two women stood there holding on to each other, not wanting to let go.

"I hope Zander makes it back in time for my wedding. I'm getting married tomorrow," Shari said sadly.

"He'll be here," Mara said, giving her a reassuring smile.

"Do you really think I'd miss your wedding?" Zander's voice asked behind them, and Shari sprung around, squealing with delight.

"Zander," she cried and ran to him. Mara watched them as they hugged each other. As she looked at them, she realized that bringing them together was the one thing she didn't regret about being here. She had watched their relationship bloom into something beautiful and wholesome.

"I wanted to make sure you both got my presents." He handed them small gift bags. Shari took hers, excited. Mara made no move to take the one he offered her. She didn't want anything from him.

"Mara?" Shari widened her eyes at her, nodding toward the gift. Reluctantly, she took the bag.

"Let's open them at the same time," Shari said, and she pulled her over to a table, sitting down. She gazed at Zander to find him watching her, a slight smile curving his lips. She wondered what he was up to. He sure as hell couldn't buy her with whatever was in the bag.

"You didn't have to do this," she started to object.

"Mara, just open it," Shari insisted. Mara obliged, pulling a blue box from the tissue paper. She opened it to reveal the diamond-and-platinum earrings and solitaire necklace she had helped him pick out at Tiffany's. Stunned, Mara looked at him.

"I can't take this!" She closed the box and put it back in the bag. He thought he could buy her with expensive jewelry? Well, he was wrong.

"It's rude to refuse a gift," Shari said as she opened the box to reveal the pearl earrings and matching necklace. "Oh, Zander, thank you," she cried and jumped up to hug her brother again. "This is so perfect."

"I'm glad you like it." He smiled.

"I love it." Shari beamed. Mara was glad she was happy about it. But she would not let him buy her. No way.

Mara got up to leave, but Zander took hold of her arm, stopping her. She looked at him furious.

"We need to talk," he insisted.

"We have nothing to talk about."

"Could you give us a minute?" he said to Shari. Shari picked up both bags and hurried off.

Mara's heart raced at being left alone with him. She didn't want him near her.

"I'm going to miss you," he leaned toward her and whispered in her ear. A shiver of raw desire raced through her. She would not let him seduce her again. Not when he was also with Tanya. She closed her eyes and hardened her heart.

"I don't think you will," she said to him with contempt.

His brows wrinkled with confusion. "Why would you say that?"

"Don't play games with me, Zander."

"Do I look like I'm playing with you?"

She pursed her lips, frustrated with him. "Yes, you have been from day one. And I was stupid enough to fall for it."

"What?" he said, confused. But Mara knew better—she wasn't about to fall for that one. He was good at playing the innocent, but she was a lot smarter now.

"In a few days, I'll be done here, so let's not complicate things any more than they already are."

"What did I do?" he asked, torn.

"You know what you did!"

"Why don't you enlighten me?" he demanded.

This was going nowhere and she was tired of it all. "Look, I leave in two days and I'm never going to see you again, so why bother? What we had was fun, but it's over." She yanked her arm from his and walked away.

Zander still did not understand why Mara was acting the way she was. After their time in Manhattan, he had decided to ask her to stay. He needed to spend more time with her. There was so much more he wanted to do with her. He wanted to show her things, take her places, and make endless love to her. He had hoped that their time in Manhattan would have enticed her to the point that when he asked her to stay, she would have. But now he didn't know what was going on with her. She was angry about something and he didn't know what it was. But he intended to find out.

In the bathroom Mara splashed cold water on her face and willed herself not to cry. Raven walked in and Mara tried not to look at her. She didn't want her to read the turmoil going on inside her. Raven came over to her and Mara knew she could read her thoughts; she felt it, for some strange reason.

"You're mad at him, I see," Raven commented as she washed her hands.

"I hate him."

"No, you don't."

"I can't deal with this." Tears burned her eyes. She felt like her world was about to fall apart.

"It's called love, and no one said it would be easy."

"I don't love him," she denied. A cold shiver raced through her and she suddenly realized that Raven was right, and it hurt like hell. Love wasn't supposed to feel like this. "I can't love him. I hate him," she cried, her voice cracking.

"No, you don't. You're just upset right now."

"I can't wait to leave this place," she said.

"You don't really mean that," Raven told her with a soft smile on her face.

"I do mean it." She knew Raven meant well, but she was wrong this time.

Raven cocked her head and studied her before responding. "You really should listen to him, and stop being so angry."

"I don't want to hear anything from him."

"Things are not always what they seem." Raven took her hands and looked deep into her eyes. She smiled at her, then kissed Mara on the cheek and left the bathroom. She stood before the mirror, staring at her now-red eyes. She felt drained and alone. She didn't know what to do. If only she hadn't been stupid enough to fall in love with Zander.

It was almost one in the morning and Mara couldn't sleep, kicking the sheets off. She headed downstairs to get some warm milk. She knew cognac would put her out faster, but Zander was home and she couldn't risk going into his library. He was probably working in there, anyway. She quietly made her way downstairs. As she passed the library, the door opened and Zander stepped out. Her heart raced at the sight of him. His hair was loose around his shoulders and his stubble made him look distinguished. He wore loose cotton pants and a matching shirt that was rumpled. She couldn't be attracted to him after all he had done. This was insane.

"We still need to talk," he stated.

"We have nothing to talk about."

"Just get the hell in here!" Mara was taken aback by his tone. She glared at him, offended. "Please?" he pleaded.

She remembered what Raven said and stood her ground. Maybe this time he would come clean about Tanya so she could have some closure. She walked past him and the inviting, cool scent of his cologne wrapped around her senses, bringing back memories of being in his arms. She suppressed the desire that raced through her. She didn't—and would not—want him.

Inside the library, Mara jumped when he slammed the door behind him. She quickly turned to look at him to find him mere inches from her. She took a big step backwards and almost fell over the armchair. Instantly he grabbed her around the waist, breaking her fall and bringing her closer to him than she really needed to be. He held her close to his body, her breasts pressed against his chest. She closed her eyes against the desire that raced through her. She kept her eyes on his chest, afraid to look at him, afraid he'd see the desire in her eyes. She started to push him away, but he pulled her gently against him and buried his face into her neck. The sudden intimate move sent shivers down her spine and made her wet. She was such a weakling when it came to him. She tried to focus, but she was too aware of her intense need for him.

"Mara," he whispered against her neck. His breath was warm, his lips soft against her flesh. She wanted to push him away, but she couldn't. It felt too good to be in his arms. His body heat surrounded her, wrapping her in its welcoming warmth. He caressed her back, pulling her closer, until she was pressed firmly against him. She could hear his heart beating rapidly. Her arms were trapped between their bodies. She wanted to wrap her arms around him and hold him to her forever. He caressed her neck with his lips and she was lost. She wanted him so much.

His mouth covered hers in a scorching kiss and

she lost all reasoning. All she knew was that she wanted him. She wanted him so badly it hurt. He moaned softly as she returned his kiss. His arms loosened a bit and she wrapped her arms around his neck. His tongue slipped into her mouth, caressing hers. She welcomed the taste of him. Her heart sang and she knew she would never love any other man the way she loved Zander Tuskcan. His touch brought her body to life. He cupped and caressed her breasts through her thin nightgown. She moaned as her nipples hardened under his fingers.

He pulled away, looking down at her, his eyes heavy with desire, and she knew she couldn't refuse him. She reached up and started to unbutton his shirt, easing it over his broad shoulders. She ran her hands over his chest and down his stomach. She loved his body, so bronze and smooth. She placed small kisses on his chest and down his stomach.

"Mara, I need you," he moaned, and she looked into his eyes. He reached down and pulled her nightgown over her head. She stood before him, in her pink cotton panties. "God, you're beautiful."

He smiled down at her. She reached for the buttons on his pants and started to undo them. Slowly she undressed him, filling her eyes with the sight of his sculptured body. He lifted her off her feet and took her over to the sofa, where he gently laid her down. He knelt beside her and slowly ran his hands over her breasts and down her stomach. She quivered under his touch. He slipped his hand inside her panties and she opened up to him. He caressed her gently as he lowered his head to her breasts. Mara moaned with pleasure as his wet, warm mouth suckled her hungrily.

"Please, Zander, I want you in me," she told him, and gasped as a finger entered her, caressing her until she was a quivering mess.

He pulled her panties off quickly, put a condom on, and covered her with his body. Mara bit her lips and moaned in sheer pleasure as he filled her. He lavished kisses all over her face and breasts. She gripped his hair, crying his name. Suddenly he sat up, taking her with him. He sat back on the sofa as he adjusted her body on top of his. She dug her nails into his shoulders as he filled her. He took her face into his hands, looking into her eyes as he thrust up into her. She moaned loudly, gripping his hair and looking down into his black eyes. She kissed him as she moved on top of him. He gripped her hips, assisting her movements. Their eyes met and held as they pleased each other, and Mara had never felt so close to any man as she did him at that moment.

She was wrapped in Zander's arms. Their bodies were covered in sweat and their hearts had finally found peace. She sighed, wishing she could be with him like this forever, but she knew better. They could never be together, however she savored the moment, inhaling his scent and caressing his damp body.

"Mara, stay with me—don't go back to D.C. I'll give you anything you want, just don't leave."

Stunned, Mara looked into his face. Was he serious? The look in his eyes said he was. He couldn't be. He wanted her to be his mistress. Was that how he saw her? The thought of it shocked her. She sat up, wrapping her arms about her naked body. She was shaking. Suddenly she felt ashamed and disgusted with herself. Was he really asking her what she thought he was? She had given in to him so easily—no wonder he thought of her the way he did. She found her nightgown and quickly pulled it on. She had to get away from him. What the hell had she been thinking, allowing him to seduce her again? She couldn't find her panties. She held on to her tears. She cursed herself for being a fool once again. She had to get away from him.

"Mara, please answer me." Mara stopped searching for her panties and looked at him. He really thought she'd stay here with him, like this. She recalled what Tanya had told her, and she was consumed with disgust. "Will you stay with me?" he insisted.

"No!"

"Why?"

"Is that all you see me as?"

"What?"

"A mistress."

"My mistress?" He looked confused. He got up and started to walk over to her. She backed away from him. His magnificent naked body was alluring, but she closed her eyes so she could focus.

"Am I supposed to be flattered that you want me as your mistress? I guess you consider that a step up for a woman like me, right?"

"Mara, that's not what I meant." He moved toward her.

"Please don't touch me!" she snapped.

"You weren't objecting before." His tone was harsh.

"I really need to get the hell away from you. God,

what's wrong with me? Why the hell did I let this happen again?" She was angry—mostly with herself—for letting things get so out of hand.

"Why are you doing this? I thought we had something special." He looked so innocent. He was such a damn good actor.

"Special." She laughed dryly.

"Yes."

"There's nothing special about us and there never will be!" she yelled and ran from the room without looking back as he called out her name.

In her room, she crawled under the covers as the tears fell. He wanted her to be his mistress. The thought of being any man's mistress made her sick to her stomach. His proposal was like a slap in the face. It made her feel cheap and it hurt like hell. She should never have given in to her carnal desires. A few more days and she'd never see him again. Mara took as much comfort in that as she could.

Chapter 24

Shari's dress was an off-the-shoulder white satin and French lace gown with a long train. Her head-piece was trimmed with pearls accented by a shimmering veil. She wore the pearls that Zander had given her. Mara fixed her veil and stood back looking at her. She made a very beautiful bride.

"Now, you're ready," she said to Shari, who turned to look at herself in the three-way mirror and smiled. Mara stood beside her and they looked at each other in the mirror. Mara's dress was lavender with a dipping, beaded neckline and a straight A-line skirt that fell to her ankles. She also wore the jewelry that Zander had given her.

Shari took her hand, squeezing tightly. "Thanks for being here with me."

"You know I wouldn't miss it for the world. Ready?" Mara asked.

Shari smiled broadly. "Ready."

Mara moved to the door of the adjoining room. She tapped, then let herself in. Zander stood adjusting his tux in the mirror. He looked very handsome. His hair was pulled back and banded by a black leather hair strap. Luc sat patiently in a chair.

"She's ready," she announced, and went back to Shari.

The wedding was absolutely beautiful. Luc, then Zander, walked Shari down the aisle, as Raven sang. Shari and Patrick exchanged vows while Mara tried her best not to look at Zander. He never stopped staring at her. As Shari and Patrick proclaimed their love for each other, Mara wished them well. She prayed for their continued happiness and for God to bless them with the babies she knew Shari was looking forward to.

After the service the bridal party headed to a botanical garden nearby where they had pictures taken. Mara did her best to ignore Zander as they posed for pictures together. She kept a smile on her face, refuseing to let Shari see her unhappiness.

At the reception hall the entire wedding party was introduced. After countless toasts, Patrick and Shari whirled onto the dance floor.

Zander came over to her and held his hand out to her to dance. Mara didn't want to, but when she saw Shari smiling at her from the dance floor, she accepted. As Zander pulled her close, she stilled her heart and body against him. She thought of him and Tanya and she stiffened, praying for the song to end.

Her mother and Henry danced by, and she smiled at them. Zander pulled her closer. She tried to pull away, but he held her firmly against him.

He looked over at his sister and Patrick as they danced beside them.

"They look happy, don't they?"

"Yes, they do," she replied looking up at him. "I guess my vacation ends tonight," she commented and diverted her eyes. She caught sight of Franklin, Patrick's younger brother, coming toward them and she smiled at him. He was the distraction she needed.

Franklin asked her to dance, and reluctantly, Zander gave her up. Mara was grateful to be out of his arms. While they danced, Franklin told her about his new girlfriend. Her advice to him was to be honest and not play with his girlfriend's feelings. Franklin promised he wouldn't.

Mara returned to the table to see Zander and Shari dancing. Shari smiled proudly at her brother as he twirled her about the dance floor.

Patrick claimed her for a dance and they ended up dancing side by side with Zander and Shari. Patrick reclaimed his wife and once again Mara found herself in Zander's arms. She looked everywhere but at Zander, fearing she'd fall under his seductive spell again.

Then she saw her. Tanya. She was dressed in a mustard dress that showed off her slim figure and ample chest. Zander must have felt her stiffen and looked in the direction that she was looking.

"Your woman is here," Mara said between clenched teeth. He looked at Tanya, then back at her with a confused expression. Angry, Mara pushed away from him and walked off.

Zander watched Mara as she walked away from him. He had told her it was over with him and Tanya. Did Mara really think he was still seeing

Tanya? Obviously she did. No wonder she kept rejecting him. He looked at Tanya to find her smiling sweetly at him. What the hell was she up to? Had she said something to Mara? He wouldn't put it past her.

Mara got herself a drink and went in search of her mother and Henry. She found them in the garden, kissing passionately. A bit embarrassed at seeing them like that, she went back inside. She decided to focus on all the happiness around her and not think about Zander and Tanya.

Mara was having a drink with Raven and Luc when she saw Stone and Tanya coming toward them. So she had come here with Stone. Tanya had a wicked grin on her face, and Mara would have loved nothing more that to slap it off.

"Mara, it's good to see you again. You look wonderful," Stone said and kissed her cheek. Tanya pulled him back roughly. Stone glanced at her, annoyed.

"Thank you, Stone."

Stone greeted Raven and Luc. Raven regarded Tanya with a peculiar look. "Yes, how are you?" Raven asked.

"Fine as always," she said, and then turned to Stone. "Darling, I need a drink," she said, and dragged him off before he could finish excusing himself.

"Never knew what Zander saw in her," Raven said with a scowl.

Mara pinched the brim of her nose as she felt a headache coming on. This was all starting to get to her. She needed to go home. She needed to get away from this madness.

"Are you all right, dear?" Raven asked, and Mara smiled at her as best she could. She had to keep it together, no matter what.

"Yes, I'm fine. It's just been an emotional day, that's all." Raven looked at her, concerned. She reassured her she'd be OK.

Shari was about to throw the bouquet when Tanya suddenly appeared, right beside Mara. Mara moved away, but Tanya kept following her. Shari threw the bouquet. It was coming right at her when Tanya elbowed her, catching the bouquet. Disappointment filled Shari's eyes when she saw who had caught the bouquet. She looked at Shari and Mara winked at her, letting her know it was OK. Shari smiled.

The garter was thrown and Zander actually caught it. Mara steeled her heart as she watched Zander put the garter on Tanya's long legs. Tanya was enjoying every minute of the attention she was getting. With the garter on, everyone cheered, and Tanya seized that moment to kiss Zander. The photographer was right there to take the picture.

"I have a favor to ask," Shari said as they fussed over each other in the bathroom, freshening up.

"Sure, anything."

"I want you to stay here until I get back from my honeymoon. Consider it an extended vacation. I'm sure Janice and Henry would love it."

"I can't," she answered quickly. She'd leave tonight if she could. She needed to get away from Zander.

"I'm not ready to say good-bye to you, especially on my wedding day. Please, Mara, I'd love for you to be here when I get back. Who's to say when you'll ever come visit me again?"

"I can't, Shari. I'm going home with my mother and Henry tomorrow. I'm sorry."

"Is it Zander?"

"No, I just need to get back to my life. It's been fun and I'm glad I came, but I really have to go home."

"I'm gonna miss you," Shari said tearfully.

"I'm missing you already."

Zander got himself a drink, upset that he hadn't seen Tanya's kiss coming. The look on Mara's face revealed pure hate and hurt. Mara already thought that they were still together. Tanya's actions had made things even worse. He just didn't know what else he could do about Mara. He had asked her to stay with him and had somehow insulted her. He just didn't get her.

He downed his drink, and reached for another. Raven joined him and started to wipe the traces of Tanya's lipstick off the corner of his mouth.

"Thanks," he mumbled.

"She's leaving." Raven gave him a slight smile.

"I know," he said, distraught.

"You didn't handle this the way I thought you would," she scolded.

"What was I supposed to do?" He looked to Raven for an answer.

"Tell her how you feel. Tell her you love her."

Zander looked at Raven, stunned. Had he heard Raven right? Was he really in love with Mara?

"You are in love with her and she needs to know that."

Raven was right. He was in love with Mara. He hadn't thought it was possible to love a woman in such a short time, but he had fallen for her in the worst way. But she wasn't in love with him, and that scared him.

"She doesn't love me."

"You don't know that." She patted his cheek, smiled, and left him to his thoughts.

An hour later, everyone waved as the limousine with Shari and Patrick pulled away. Mara's mother had an arm about her waist.

"It was such a lovely wedding," her mother commented.

"It surely was," Henry agreed.

"So, should I be planning a wedding for you two?" Mara asked. Henry looked at Janice and smiled.

"We were thinking Vegas," Henry said.

"Vegas? I don't think de' reverend would like that."

"He can come along if he wants to," Henry teased, and her mother laughed. It was good to see her mother laughing the way she did. Mara turned and walked away. She had to hold it together.

The wedding guests were starting to leave and it was time she did the same. She was in the dressing room, packing the wedding cases, when her mother walked in.

"Yu' OK?" she asked, moving up to her.

"I can't wait to get out of here so I can find a job and take care of you." She sighed heavily.

"When yu' goin' to stop?"

"What are you talking about?"

"When yu' goin' to live yu' life an' stop worryin' 'bout mine? Yu' don't intend to get married an' have a family one day?"

"Yes," Mara answered timidly.

"So why yu' spend so much time worryin' about me?"

"You're my mother and I love you."

"I love yu' too, but I don't want yus' givin' up yu' life for me. In case yu' don't notice, I'm doin' ju' fine with Henry. Yu' need to stop worryin' 'bout me and worry 'bout yu'self."

"Everything I do is because of you," Mara said softly.

Janice took her by the shoulders and looked her square in the eyes. "An' I appreciate it, but yu' have to live yu' life. Yu' lettin' a lot of good t'ings pass yu' by. Yu' need to stop it."

Mara suddenly realized that her mother was right. She had focused so hard on taking care of her mother her whole life, she hadn't lived at all. She had chosen computer science as a major in college because it guaranteed a good career, which meant a better life for her mother. Now, her mother was telling her to move on with her life, without her. Mara was suddenly confused and very afraid. She never thought they'd ever be apart.

Her mother moved up to her and pulled her into her arms, hugging her tightly.

"I know it's been hard with jus' me an' yu', but it's time for yu' to live yu' life. I want yu' to be happy."

"I can't do that without you," she cried.

"Yes, yu' can.

"But everything was for you."

"But everyt'ing was to make yu' a better person, so I wouldn't have to worry 'bout yu'. I'm very proud of yu'—yu' have never disappointed me."

Mara knew her mother was proud of her. It was that knowledge that drove her in life. She never wanted her mother to be disappointed in her.

"I jus' want yu' to be happy."

"I am." Mara wiped at her tears.

"No, yu' not—I see it in yu' eyes. Yu' have to find yu' happiness."

"I will."

"Good," Janice said. "Yu' finish up here an' come downstairs."

"OK." She watched as her mother left. Her mother was right. She needed to start to live her own life. Janice had moved on with Henry and it was time she did the same. Once she got home, everything would be different, everything. She had a future to look forward to, and hopefully, along the way she'd find the right man. She picked up the makeup case and left the room. In the hallway she found Tanya just outside the door, obviously waiting for her.

"What the hell do you want now?" Mara really wasn't in the mood for her crap.

"Isn't it time you left?"

"Don't start with me," Mara warned.

Tanya's eyes narrowed with hate. Mara couldn't wait to get the hell out of New Jersey and away from Zander and this psycho bitch.

Mara shook her head and started toward the stairs. Tanya suddenly grabbed her by the arm. Her fingernails dug into her skin. Mara winced in pain. "What the . . ."

"He's mine," Tanya snapped. "He'll always be mine. You're just some convenient little whore for the moment. Well, your moment is up. Get the hell out!"

Mara calmly looked down at Tanya's hand, then back at her. "Let me go, or I won't be responsible for what I'll do to you!"

Tanya let her go, but smiled wickedly. "He's mine, he'll always be mine. Even when you are gone."

"That's good for you now, isn't it?"

"Why don't you just leave?"

"I guess it must be healthy nowadays to obsess over a man who can never love you."

Tanya reared back, raising her hand. Mara punched her in the arm that came at her. Tanya cried out in pain, grabbing her arm.

"I suggest you don't start anything with me," Mara told her, ready to beat the hell of out her. She stopped and took a deep breath. She would not let this woman drive her to violence.

"He can't stay away from me. Haven't you realized that yet?" Tanya laughed. "I mean, we were in Atlanta together, or did he fail to tell you that? Then again, maybe he told you what you wanted to hear, so he could get some." Tanya looked her up and down in disgust.

Mara's chest heaved in anger. Mara took a step back from Tanya, realizing that she was right. The knowledge of it hurt like hell. Zander had played her for the fool she was.

"Do you really think a man like Zander would ever want a low-class nothing like you?" Tanya continued.

Mara looked her straight in the eye and said, "Apparently he did last night."

Tanya's eyes went deathly cold. Mara laughed with some satisfaction and headed for the stairs. The sooner she got away from here, the better. She couldn't take much more of this drama. She started down the stairs.

"He's mine, you bitch!" Tanya cried out, directly behind her. Mara turned quickly, but she wasn't quick enough. Tanya's hands slammed into her chest. Mara went flying backwards.

Mara screamed as she lost her balance, falling. She twisted, trying to regain her footing, but she couldn't. A searing pain ripped through her ankle and her back slammed into the wall. She tried to grip on to the railing, but it was too far away. Somewhere she hit her head, and an even more mind-bending pain tore through her. Everything went black.

Zander was outside, talking with Janice and Henry, when he heard a shrill scream from inside. He rushed back into the hall. His heart was racing. Something bad had happened—he could feel it in his bones. He ran into the foyer to see a small group of guests huddled at the foot of the stairs. He pushed his way through the crowd and what he saw made his heart stop. It took him a full few seconds before he could breathe.

Mara was at the foot of the stairs, on the ground, facedown, and she wasn't moving.

Janice was right behind him. She took one look at Mara and screamed. "Oh God—Mara!" They got to Mara at the same time. Zander started to turn her over.

"Don't!" Luc's voice stopped him. "Don't move her—you might cause more damage. Let me take a look at her." Zander moved back a bit, watching as Luc examined her. Why wasn't she moving? What had happened to her? Zander could feel tears in his eyes. A moment ago she was fine, now she was lying here, not moving.

"What happened to her?" he asked, as he watched Luc inspect Mara's neck. She moaned softly and her eyes fluttered, but then she went still.

"What happened to me baby?" Janice started to panic. Zander put his arms around her, comforting her.

"She fell down the stairs," Tanya said. "I saw it—she tripped." Everyone paused to look at her.

"No, she didn't, you pushed her. I saw you," Raven responded. A shocked gasp went through the crowd. Panic filled Tanya's eyes as she looked around the room.

"No, no, you're wrong," she cried frantically.

"Someone call an ambulance," Luc said.

"Oh God, my baby," Janice moaned. "Why?"

Zander stared at Tanya in disbelief. "How could you do this?" He moved toward her. He grabbed her by the shoulders and shook her.

"I—I," Tanya stuttered.

"Get out of my sight!" Zander whispered sharply before shoving her away from him. Tanya let out a sharp gasp and ran from the room.

Zander returned his attention to Mara's unmoving body. Janice was crying in Henry's arms.

Luc continued to attend to Mara. "Will she be OK?" Zander asked. The fear of losing her overwhelmed him. He had to think positively. She was going to be all right.

"Nothing seems to be broken, but we won't know until she wakes up."

He could not lose her. He had just found her.

Mara could hear voices, but she just couldn't open her eyes. She tried to move, but the pain ripped through her. She sank back into the warm darkness, hearing her mother's voice calling her name.

Chapter 25

Mara woke up to a white ceiling. Was she dead? She couldn't be. She closed her eyes, then opened them again. The white ceiling had a water spot, and someone was holding her hand. She wasn't dead. Thank God.

"Hey, baby." Her mother's soothing voice reached her. She turned her head to see her mother, sitting by her, holding her hand. Mara tried to smile, but she felt drowsy. Her mouth was so dry.

"Where am I?" she managed.

"The hospital."

"Am I going to be OK?" She noticed her mother was still in the dress she had on at the wedding. She wondered how long she'd been in the hospital.

"Yes, thank God," Janice told her.

"You'll be fine. All you have is a sprained ankle and some bruises." Zander's voice drew her attention. She looked to her left to see him. His eyes were soft with concern. Why did he even care? she wondered. Mara looked away from him to Henry, who sat in a chair nearby. Henry smiled at her. She noticed that they were all still in their wedding gear.

"I'm thirsty." Mara cleared her dry throat.

"We know Tanya pushed you down the stairs," Zander said. "If you want to press charges against her, it's understandable." He actually looked guilty.

"Charges?"

"She did push you down the stairs. Worse could have happened," Zander insisted.

"Well, it didn't, thank God." She coughed. "You just keep your crazy woman in check, and away from me." Her cough got worse.

"Here, baby, drink this." Her mother brought a cup with a straw to her lips. Mara took a long sip—it relieved her dry cough.

"When can I leave?" Mara wanted to go home to D.C.

"Let me get the doctor," Henry said and hurried from the room.

Mara closed her eyes. "What time is it and how long have I been here?"

"Less than an hour," Zander answered. Mara kept her eyes closed, wishing she were in D.C. and away from him. He had caused her nothing but pain; now it was physical because of his woman.

"Mara, I'm sorry," he started.

"Please don't," she moaned, cutting him off.

The doctor, a tall, thin white man about fifty, walked in. Henry was right behind him. The doctor picked up her chart and reviewed it.

"Ms. Evans, you can go home," the doctor told her with a smile.

"Thank you." She smiled at the doctor. "Why am I so drowsy?"

"It's the painkillers we gave you. They will wear off soon. I want you to take it easy for a while. Keep that ankle wrapped tight and stay off it for a while. Also, keep it elevated. And if you get any headaches, see a doctor immediately," he informed her.

"Thank you, Doctor." Mara closed her eyes, then opened them to see Zander walking out of the room behind the doctor.

"That Tanya is crazy," her mother exclaimed the minute Zander was out of the room. "What Zander doin' with a crazy woman like that?"

"You'd have to ask him."

"So why she push yu'?" her mother asked, and Mara sighed tiredly.

"Because I sorta moved in on her territory."

"What happen' between yu' an' Zander?"

"Nothing. He had fun, now he's back to her. She got mad and I ended up in here." If she had known better, she would never have gotten involved with him.

"He can't do that to yu'!" Her mother's voice rose in pitch.

"Janice!" Henry warned. Her mother looked at Henry and frowned.

"Mama, don't be upset. I knew what I was doing. I was just stupid to think a man like him would actually want someone like me."

"What's wrong with yu'?" Janice asked, offended.

"Mama, look at how they live. Do you really think a man like Zander would be with a woman like me? Education or not, I'm not in his class and I never will be."

Her mother shook her head, obviously disappointed.

"Don't say that," Henry told her. "You are a beautiful, educated woman. You have a lot to offer any man."

Mara gazed at him and smiled, welcoming his words of praise. "Thanks, but I fooled myself with him more than once, and I've paid the price. I can't wait to go home."

Henry and Janice looked at each other, concerned.

Zander entered the room and instantly knew something was wrong. The tension was thick. The look on Janice's face was one of contempt—he wondered what Mara had said to her. He knew it wasn't good, and that frustrated him. Mara was crying and it tore at his heart.

"Are you all right?" he asked. He took Mara's hand in his. She pulled her hand away roughly and wiped her tears. Zander was at a loss, and he couldn't figure out what to do. She was hurting to the point that she was crying in front of her mother and Henry. He knew he was the cause of her pain somehow; what he didn't know was how to fix it. He had to do something or he'd lose her. When his cell phone rang, they all looked at him. This was not the time. He sighed and quickly answered it.

Mara turned her head away as Zander answered his cell phone. She couldn't stand being in the same room with him. She wished he would just leave. She didn't want to see him, smell his cologne, or hear his voice. It brought back too many memories. She just wanted to forget it all.

"What, no—oh my God! Is she OK?" she heard him ask. Mara looked at him, alarmed. Her first thought was of Shari.

"Is Shari OK?" Mara asked, concerned.

He wore a horrified look on his face. He looked at her as he turned off his phone. She knew something horrible had happened. Fear raced through her.

"What is it?"

"It's Tanya," he said.

Mara swallowed the anger that suddenly rose within her, making her want to vomit. Once again it was about Tanya. She was sick of him and Tanya.

"What about Tanya?" Henry asked.

"She was in a car accident. I have to call her family," he said, and hurried from the room. Mara felt her heart shatter into a thousand pieces. He was running to the woman who had hurt her. He still loved her. She turned her face into the pillow and willed herself not to cry. He was not worth it.

Her mother sat by her side. She took her into her arms and held her as she cried.

"I want to go home, Mama," she said between sobs.

"Yes, I know, baby." She rocked her until her tears stopped. Mara hated Zander for doing this to her. She hated herself for letting it happen.

Two days later, Mara hugged Helen tightly at the front door. Her mother and Henry had already said good-bye and were waiting in the car that would take them to the airport.

"I'm going to miss you." She kissed Helen's

cheek. Helen had tears in her eyes—she tried to smile but couldn't.

"Are you sure you have to go so early?"

"Yes."

"I'm glad you came. It's been so wonderful having you here."

"Thank you, Helen. Thank you for everything. Kiss your grandson for me, and you take care."

"What should I tell Zander? He'll be home from Manhattan tonight." Zander had been in Manhattan the past two days, which had made it easy for her to pack and get ready to leave.

"He knows I'm leaving," Mara lied. Helen looked at her sadly. Mara hadn't seen Zander since the hospital episode. Tanya was in some car accident. Mara didn't doubt it was another one of her games to get Zander to run to her, and he had. The next day he had left on his business trip. A part of her was glad she hadn't seen Zander since; it made leaving a lot easier.

"Don't be a stranger."

"I'll try not to be." Mara knew there was no way she'd ever come back to this house. Patrick and Shari would have their own house soon, so even if she did come back to visit, she wouldn't have to see Zander.

Chapter 26

Mara spent the next week resting at home. She wanted her ankle to heal properly before she scheduled any job interviews. She went through her wardrobe to see what she had. She had taken all the clothes that Shari had bought her in New Jersey, but they were mostly social outfits, so she couldn't really use them for interviews. As she started to look over the two decent skirts and pants that she had, she realized that she really could use a few suits, but she had no money to buy any.

She remembered her church sister, Kay Frank, who just had twins, talking about giving away her business suits. Kay had quit her job at a law firm to raise her kids. Mara decided to give her a call—they were about the same size. Kay told her to come pick up the suits the next day. Mara couldn't thank her enough.

It was almost midnight, and her mother still wasn't home. If she hadn't seen her going into Henry's house four hours ago, she would have called the police already. Mara was so pissed at her mother for being over at Henry's house that late, she couldn't sleep. She knew they were seeing each other, but she should have at least had the decency to call.

Mara heard the keys turn in the lock. "Yu' OK?" her mother asked, concerned. She closed the door behind her.

"You could have called—I was worried."

"I was with Henry," her mother told her, putting down her bag and looking at her strangely.

"You could have called."

Janice frowned at her. "Am I yu' child."

Mara didn't know what to say, so she hung her head. Her mother walked over to her and sat down.

"If yu' was so worried, why didn't yu' just call over Henry's."

Mara looked up her mother. "Excuse me for looking out for you," Mara snapped.

"OK, enough of that attitude. Why yu' so upset? Yu' been sulking' aroun' the house all week. What's really wrong with yu'?"

"Nothing."

"Look at me," her mother demanded. She looked at her, holding back her tears. "Yu' miss Zander?"

"No!"

"Why yu' lyin'?"

"I'm not lying," Mara snapped.

She did miss Zander in the worst way. She had left a huge chunk of her heart with that man, and it hurt. She had tried not to think of him, but it was impossible. She dreamt of him every night. He haunted her every thought; then the pain of his using her would set in, tearing at her heart.

"It's OK to miss him. It's natural—yu' love him."

"I—I don't love him," she denied forcefully.

"Remember, I know when yu' lyin'," Janice said, and Mara fell into her mother's arms, crying. Her mother smelled of Henry's Old Spice cologne. She pulled away from her.

"Were you just with Henry?" she asked, stunned. She knew they were spending more and more time with each other, but sex? Her mother was having sex? She was too old to be having sex. She didn't even want to think about it.

"Yu' were with Zander," her mother pointed out.

"That's different," she stuttered. She couldn't believe her mother had just had sex.

"How so? 'Cause yu' young, an' Henry an' me old?"

Mara opened her mouth to say something, but she couldn't think of anything to say. Her mother was right, and she had no right to judge her. She was happy her mother had found love. She had lived her life without the love of a man for a long time. So why was Mara tripping? New Jersey had left her too emotional.

"I guess I'm just jealous," she admitted.

"Jealous? Why?"

"I feel like I'm losing you."

"Yu'll never lose me."

"What's going to happen when you marry Henry and move out of my life?" She wiped at her tears.

"I'll neva' be out of yu' life, baby. I'm yu' mother—a mother can never be out of her child's life, especially one like yu'. Yu' very special to me. I love yu'."

"I love you, too."

"One day yu' goin' to find true love, an' get married an' give me some grandkids to play with."

"One day," she mused with a slight smile.

"I'm sorry t'ings didn't work with yu' an' Zander."

She sighed deeply and said, "I'm sorry, too, but he lied, and I can't trust a man that's going to lie to me." It would take time, but she would forget him.

"Yu' deserve the best. Yu' know that?"

"I know." She forced a smile.

"An' yu'll have it, too, yu'll see."

"Thanks, Mama," she said, and hugged her mother close. She would never see Zander again. It was time she let go and moved on. If her mother could do it, then so could she. It was the only way she'd be happy again.

Chapter 27

Zander was like a zombie. He couldn't concentrate on anything. He felt like he had lost a part of him. He missed Mara. He had difficulties sleeping at night, tormented with thoughts of her. He never thought any woman could hurt him like his ex-wife, but this was worse. He felt like she had taken his heart with her when she left. He was a mess and he didn't know what to do. He wished Shari was here, but she had called, telling him that she and Patrick were extending their honeymoon in Hawaii. He didn't tell her about Tanya pushing Mara down the stairs. She sounded so happy and he didn't want to spoil it. He would tell her once she got back. He needed Mara so much it hurt.

"Why don't you call her?" Raven suddenly asked. Zander lifted his head from his desk to see Raven in the doorway. She smiled and entered the library. It was good to see her. He hugged her and kissed her cheek.

"You look like hell," Raven told him, pushing him away. She rubbed his unshaven cheek.

"I know," he moaned.

"I see you let her go."

"I couldn't hold on to her."

Raven shook her head, disappointed.

"She hates me."

"No, she doesn't. She's just upset."

"She confuses me," Zander said. "I only knew her for such a short time and look at me. How the hell could this happen?" He was angry—angry for loving another woman who didn't love him in return. He thought he'd have learned his lesson.

"It doesn't take four weeks for a man or a woman to fall in love."

"She doesn't care about me." He dropped onto the sofa. Raven sat beside him.

"You can't be afraid to love, Zander, or you will be miserable for the rest of your life."

"I tried talking to her, but she didn't want to hear anything I had to say. What else is there for me to do? I can't force her to love me. I don't know what to do." Zander moaned, putting his head on Raven's shoulder. She laughed soothingly and hugged him.

"I think you know exactly what you have to do," she said confidently.

After Raven left, Zander paced his office, thinking hard. He just didn't know what to do. He thought of going to D.C. to talk to her, but he doubted if that would work. He couldn't even bring himself to pick up the phone. Maybe she needed some time to cool off. She hadn't even told him good-bye, and that bothered him.

A tap at the door paused his pacing.

"Come," he called out, and the door slowly opened to reveal Tanya. She wasn't exactly the person he wanted to see right now. She looked a lot better than the last time he had seen her, all battered and bruised in the hospital. The only sign of her accident was a small scar over her left brow.

"Can we talk?"

"If you hadn't had that accident, I would have had you arrested for what you did to Mara," he told her bluntly. He hadn't spoken to her since the accident and had refused all of her calls.

"I know." She approached him timidly.

"What do you want?"

"You hate me, don't you?" she asked seductively. Would she ever stop?

"What do you want?" he asked with contempt.

"Please don't hate me. I promise if you give me another chance I'll make you forget about her." She smiled seductively. He definitely wasn't interested in anything she had to offer.

"Is that why you're here? To make me forget about her?"

"You will forget about her with time." She sauntered over to him. He watched her closely.

"I don't want to forget about her. I'm in love with her. How the hell do you expect me to forget about the woman I want?"

Tanya's face went from shock to determination. She tossed her hair with a seductive smile. There was nothing alluring about her. She only succeeded at annoying him with her games.

"You loved me once, you can love me again," she said.

"I might have loved you, but I was never in love with you. I'm in love with Mara."

"You can't really be in love with her," she exclaimed, appalled. He looked at her long and hard. Her face contorted in disgust. "You love her?"

"Yes, I do," he stated proudly.

"What about me?"

"I'm sick and tired of your little games. Life is always some game with you. Well, your game is over. Get the hell out of my sight!"

"It's a good thing I didn't tell Sean no about joining him in Paris. I just wanted to give you another chance," she stated calmly.

"Thanks—but no, thanks," he said in disgust.

"Can't say I didn't try," she said, opening her bag. He watched as she pulled out a cell phone and tossed it at him. He caught it. It was his phone, the one he thought he lost in Atlanta.

"Where'd you get this?" he demanded.

"It served its purpose," she smiled. "Good-bye, Zander. Have a nice life," she said on her way out, laughing. Zander simply shook his head with contempt. He hoped she found whatever she was looking for in Paris. He looked at the phone. It was no use to him now. He'd had it replaced weeks ago. He tossed it onto his desk and resumed his pacing. He had to figure out a way to get Mara back.

Chapter 28

The doorbell rang a second time and Mara hurried to answer it. She bumped her ankle on the edge of the coffee table and a searing pain ripped through her leg. Damn, she did not need her ankle acting up—she had two interviews tomorrow and had to wear pumps. The doorbell rang again, and she gingerly hopped over to answer it. She pulled the door open and gasped when she saw him. Her heartbeat escalated, her throat went dry, and she couldn't speak. She could only stare at him, her mouth gaping open.

Zander was standing in her hallway. A million and one questions raced through her head. The main one was, *What was he doing here?* She never expected to see him, much less have him appear in her doorway.

God, he looked good standing there in slacks and a light sweater. So good. She suddenly became conscious of her raggedy T-shirt and old shorts. She ran her hand over her uncombed hair and pulled at her shirt. He slowly looked her over, his eyes lingering here and there. She felt herself grow warm under his scorching gaze. How could he still affect her like this? She hated him—she had to remember that. She straightened her back and looked him square in the eyes.

"What—what are you doing here?" she asked, trying to remain calm under his piercing gaze.

"Hello to you, too." He paused and waited for her to respond, but she didn't know what to say. "Can I come in?"

She stepped back, allowing him to enter, inhaling his familiar scent as he passed her. She bit her lips and stilled her body against the desire that washed over her. He turned slowly to look at her. She closed the door, leaning against it, suddenly feeling weak. He still had such a strong effect on her. He looked so out of place standing in the middle of her small living room.

"You didn't say good-bye," he said softly. His eyes held her captive.

Her heart was pounding so hard she could hear it echoing in her ears. She wanted to run from him, but where would she go? She thought she had left him for good in New Jersey; now, here he was. She was suddenly scared to death. He moved toward her. She stepped back, almost falling; he caught her around her waist and brought her close to him. She was back in his arms again, and that was how she had gotten into trouble in the first place. His overwhelming presence washed over her, and she sighed heavily. She didn't want to be so close to him. Mara pushed away, hopping to a safe distance. She couldn't think straight when he was so close.

"Your ankle is still bothering you?"

"I just bumped it on the table answering the door."

His eyes never left hers. She licked her lips nervously. His eyes fell to her mouth; he wanted to kiss her and she wanted him to. But she wouldn't let him. She couldn't. She wouldn't let herself fall into his trap again.

"I missed you," he said, and her heart raced with excitement. She didn't know what to say. She still couldn't believe that he was right here in front of her, telling her he missed her.

"Why are you here, Zander?"

"How do you say good-bye to someone, Mara?" She was stumped for a brief moment, then she remembered Tanya.

"There was nothing left to say," she whispered. When he shook his head at her, she swallowed, biting her lips.

"How do you figure that?" he demanded. She heard the anger building in his voice.

"Zander, we have nothing . . ."

"You stop right there!"

Mara could feel the tears forming in her eyes; she would not let him see her cry. She had shed enough tears since she came back to D.C. She had to be strong.

"Why are you doing this?" Her voice cracked.

"Why do you keep pushing me away? I've tried, Mara, I really have. But I can't understand why you are shutting me out."

"We were wrong," her voice trembled. "We were never meant to be."

"How can you say that?" he said, hurt.

"Because it's the truth. I know that and you know that."

He studied her calmly. She held her back straight, her fists in tight balls at her sides.

"I've never felt so close to any woman except you."

"You are such a liar!"

His eyes narrowed in surprise at her outburst.

"You really take me for a fool, don't you?"

He appeared hurt by her words, but she wasn't fooled. "I've never taken you for a fool."

"You are so full of it!"

"Why don't you just get it out of your system and tell me what the hell I did to you to make you hate me so much?" he asked sharply.

"Don't you dare stand there and pretend that you're innocent."

"Jesus, Mara, why don't you just come out and tell me what the hell I did wrong?" His eyes were blazing mad as he looked down on her.

"You said it was over with you and Tanya. You lied to me!"

"I didn't lie to you. It is over with her and me."

"You were in Atlanta with her!"

"I was not with Tanya in Atlanta. Granted, she showed up at my hotel, but I was not with her."

He expected her to believe that. "She answered your cell phone when I called you that night. So how the hell can you stand there and tell me that you weren't with her?" she screamed.

Zander looked stumped for a minute. She could see him formulating his answer. "*That's* why she had it." His explanation was contrived and too convenient.

"So you do admit that Tanya was with you?"

"Yes! No!" he stammered.

"You really take me for an idiot, don't you?"

"No, no, I don't."

"Then how the hell can you stand there and try to feed me that crap?"

"Mara, listen to me."

She shook her head. "You got what you wanted. Wasn't that your plan? To seduce me?"

"Mara, no."

"I don't want to hear anything you have to say. You're nothing but a liar. You've lied to me from day one!"

"Mara, I'm not lying to you!"

"Get out!"

"What?" He was stunned.

"Get out! I don't want you here. I don't know why you came here in the first place."

"Just listen to me."

"No, go away! You wasted your time coming here."

Suddenly he grabbed her and brought her up to him. His face was mere inches from hers. She quivered in fear when she saw the determined look in his eyes. She would not let him frighten her.

"I hate you!" she screamed. Suddenly he released her as if her words had actually burned him. "I'm sorry I ever met you." Mara was angry and she knew it was her anger talking, but all she felt was hurt. She could see him trying to hold on to his temper. He turned and stormed out.

Mara collapsed onto the sofa, buried her face in her hands, and cried. Why had she allowed him to do this to her? He had broken her heart and he was still stomping all over it. She didn't want to hear anything he had to say. Nothing he had to say would make her feel any differently.

"Do you really hate me that much?" Mara's head

snapped up at his voice. He had left—why was he back?

Zander stood over her with a determined look on his face. She wiped the tears from her cheeks.

"Do you really hate me, Mara?" His voice trembled and she saw fear in his eyes.

"Please," she moaned. She really couldn't handle any more lying from him. Her heart couldn't take it.

"Not until you answer my question truthfully."

"Please, Zander, just go," she pleaded.

"Do you really hate me, Mara?"

She looked into his sad black eyes. She didn't hate him; she loved him too much, and that was why it hurt so badly. She couldn't think straight. She thought she had dealt with her pain, but seeing him brought it all back.

"Do you hate me?"

"You really hurt me, Zander."

"Mara, I swear to God, I don't know what I did. Tell me what I did so I can make it better," he pleaded, kneeling before her.

"You said you weren't with her and you were," she sniffled.

"I wasn't." His eyes searched hers.

"I called and she answered your phone—twice."

"She took my phone when she came to my hotel room."

"I don't want to hear any more of your lies." She got up, and he pulled her back down.

"Mara, listen to me. When I came out of the shower in Atlanta, Tanya was in my room."

She covered her ears and closed her eyes, shaking her head. He pulled her hands from her ears.

"She got the clerk to let her into my room. I told her to leave and she did. She must have taken my phone then, because yesterday she gave it back to me, telling me it had served its purpose. Now I know what she meant. Don't you see? She was trying to keep us apart. Don't let her do this to us," he pleaded.

Mara heard his words, but she was afraid to believe him. She knew Tanya was ruthless, but it was too simple.

"I don't know," she told him as the tears started to roll down her cheeks. He pulled a handkerchief from his pocket and started to wipe away her tears.

"I'm in love with you," he said. His words stunned her. For a moment Mara couldn't respond. Had she heard him right? "I love you," he repeated, and Mara blinked. She had heard him right the first time.

"What did you just say?" Her heart raced like crazy.

"I said, I'm in love with you."

"God, please don't say that if you don't mean it." She started to cry again. Her heart erupted with sheer joy, but it also ached with uncertainty. "I can't believe you, I just . . ."

"You don't believe me?" He looked at her, hurt.

"I—I just can't. You can't love me. You said it yourself. You don't believe in love."

"Mara Evans, you made me believe in love. I fell for you the night you cursed at me while you drank my cognac in that short nightgown with the little flowers."

He remembered her nightgown. He had paid a great deal of attention to her that night. Her eyes searched his. There was nothing but pure love there. She'd never seen it before and it scared her. He really was in love with her.

She looked at him, wondering what future there was for them. She had to be realistic. She had to be sure of what was to come, if anything.

"You have it all. What do you want with me? I have nothing to give you and you know that," she said.

"That's where you are wrong. You have everything to give me—that I need. Who's going to do my hair while she tells me I'm full of crap?"

She laughed slightly, and shook her head. He was in love with her, or he wouldn't be here spilling his guts to her. She loved him even more.

"I have everything except the one thing I need, and that's your love. Do I have your love, Mara? Because if I don't, I will leave right now." His eyes frantically searched hers with anticipation. He cupped her face in his hands.

"I need you," he declared. Mara couldn't breathe. Her breath was caught in her throat. She felt lightheaded. She loved him with all her heart and soul, but she was so scared. She recalled her mother's words about being happy and living her life. The tears came down in streams and she brushed them away. He smiled gently and wiped at her tears.

"I love you," he told her and gently kissed her lips.

She pulled back. "Don't play with me, Zander. Please, I can't take it," she whimpered as her lips trembled.

"Look in my eyes and tell me if I look like I'm playing with you," he demanded gently.

"I don't . . ."

"I don't play games, Mara, I never have. Not when it comes to my happiness."

"We are too different," she said.

"Are we?" He wasn't making this easy for her.

"Yes. I don't come from money and I'm not exactly classy like . . ."

"Let me tell you this," he cut her off. "You are by far the classiest, sexiest, most vibrant woman I've ever been with. Before I met you, I never thought any woman could make me feel what you make me feel. I was dead inside for a long time, Mara, and then you walked in and kicked me awake."

"You are too rich for my blood," she told him.

"I didn't know my money was a factor in what you feel for me."

"Maybe."

"OK, so tell me. Are you happy here?"

"I have my mother . . ." She was a bit taken aback by his question.

"From what I've seen, your mother has made a life with Henry. Who are you going to start a new life with?"

She stared at him, speechless. He was right. Her mother had moved on after all these years. She needed to live her own life.

"I wouldn't have come all this way if I didn't truly love you. Mara, I want you in my life."

Mara's heart sang at his words. "You love me?" she asked, needing to hear him say it again.

"I never thought I'd love any woman like I do you. I'm just sorry I never told you earlier. I guess I was waiting for the right time. Of course, there's never a perfect time to tell someone that you love them. I'm lonely and empty without you, and I'm not about to let you go—do you understand that? I'm not going home without you. But my question is, do you love me?" He actually looked scared.

"Oh God, yes. More than you'll ever know," she told him, unable to hold back her excitement.

"Then tell me," he said.

"I love you, Zander Tuskcan. I love you—I love you so much."

"That's what I needed to hear." He got up and pulled her into his arms. His mouth engulfed hers in a hot, scorching kiss that left her weak. She wrapped her arms about his neck as he lifted her off her feet against him. She opened up to him like a flower, loving him with all her heart. His tongue danced over hers, making her moan. She could feel his heart beating against her breasts. Oh, how she loved this man.

Finally, Zander put her down and she gazed up at him lovingly.

"I missed you so much." She caressed his cheek. He captured her hand and pressed his lips into her palm, sending shivers down her spine.

He caressed her cheek. "I missed you, too. You think Shari's up to planning another wedding?"

"You want to, to, marry me?" She didn't expect a marriage proposal, not so soon.

Zander pulled back, looking at her seriously. "I want a woman I can spend the rest of my life with and that's going to be you. And some kids are welcome."

He wanted her to be his wife. Everything was so

different now. Here he was, loving her, needing her to complete him, as he did her. Life was strange and so wonderful. She never thought she would ever be this happy in her entire life.

"Good, so let's not waste any time. Go pack—I'm taking you home."

She blinked back her tears. "Home?"

"Yes, where you belong. With me."

"I don't believe this is happening to me," she exclaimed in glee.

"Believe it." Zander smiled and kissed her deeply before releasing her.

The front door opened and her mother and Henry walked in.

"Well, look who finally showed up," Janice commented harshly.

"I told you he'd come get her," Henry said and smiled.

"Hello, Janice. Henry," Zander greeted them, holding on to Mara's waist.

Her mother placed her hands on her hips and addressed Zander. "What took yu' so long? She's been drivin' me crazy with all that cryin' over yu'."

"Oh God, Mama, don't tell him that," she moaned, embarrassed.

"Why not? He's the one responsible for yu' sleepless nights."

Zander looked down at her. "No more crying, OK?" He kissed her briefly.

"OK."

"So, young man, what are your intentions with my future daughter?" Henry asked, and Mara wished she had a hole to crawl into.

"First, she's coming home with me to New Jersey," Zander said and gazed down at her. "Where we can plan our wedding."

"My baby gettin' married," Janice cried in glee, holding her hands out to Mara. There were tears of joy in her mother's eyes. She went to her mother, crying also.

In two months her life had done a one hundred and eighty degree turn, something she never saw coming. All she knew was that the man she loved was here for her. She was getting married—and to the man of her dreams. Nothing could be better. Mara gazed at Zander, and he mouthed to her that he loved her. Her heart took off in flight.

Check Out These Other
Dafina Novels

Sister Got Game
0-7582-0856-1

by Leslie Esdaile
$6.99US/**$9.99**CAN

Say Yes
0-7582-0853-7

by Donna Hill
$6.99US/**$9.99**CAN

In My Dreams
0-7582-0868-5

by Monica Jackson
$6.99US/**$9.99**CAN

True Lies
0-7582-0027-7

by Margaret Johnson-Hodge
$6.99US/**$9.99**CAN

Testimony
0-7582-0637-2

by Felicia Mason
$6.99US/**$9.99**CAN

Emotions
0-7582-0636-4

by Timmothy McCann
$6.99US/**$9.99**CAN

The Upper Room
0-7582-0889-8

by Mary Monroe
$6.99US/**$9.99**CAN

Got A Man
0-7582-0242-3

by Daaimah S. Poole
$6.99US/**$8.99**CAN

Available Wherever Books Are Sold!

Check out our website at www.kensingtonbooks.com.

Look For These Other
Dafina Novels

If I Could
0-7582-0131-1

by Donna Hill
$6.99US/**$9.99**CAN

Thunderland
0-7582-0247-4

by Brandon Massey
$6.99US/**$9.99**CAN

June In Winter
0-7582-0375-6

by Pat Phillips
$6.99US/**$9.99**CAN

Yo Yo Love
0-7582-0239-3

by Daaimah S. Poole
$6.99US/**$9.99**CAN

When Twilight Comes
0-7582-0033-1

by Gwynne Forster
$6.99US/**$9.99**CAN

It's A Thin Line
0-7582-0354-3

by Kimberla Lawson Roby
$6.99US/**$9.99**CAN

Perfect Timing
0-7582-0029-3

by Brenda Jackson
$6.99US/**$9.99**CAN

Never Again Once More
0-7582-0021-8

by Mary B. Morrison
$6.99US/**$8.99**CAN

Available Wherever Books Are Sold!

Check out our website at www.kensingtonbooks.com.

Grab These Other
Dafina Novels
(mass market editions)

Grab These Other
Dafina Novels
(trade paperback editions)

Grab These Other
Thought Provoking Books